GameMonster

GameMonster

David Marti

Published by David Marti
Copyright © 2010 David Marti
All Rights Reserved

Library of Congress Catalog
ISBN 978-0-578-05701-9

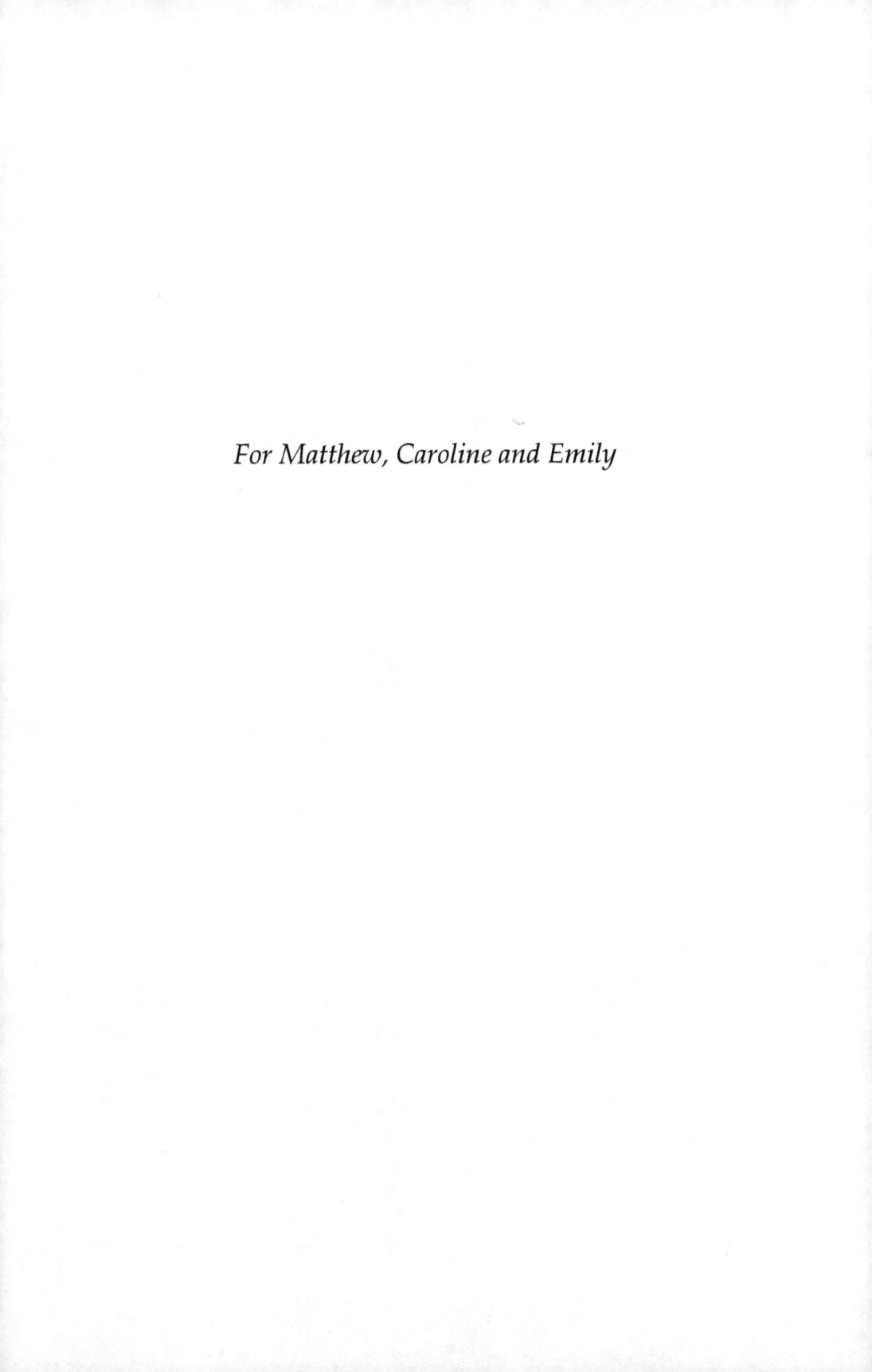

For Matthew, Caroline and Emily

READ
AT YOUR OWN
RISK!

Contents

CHAPTER ZERO

The Game Testers

A green stinkbug scurried across the highly polished floor searching for food. It skittered back and forth in nervous zigzags, twitching and clicking and pausing every few steps to check for danger. The bug skidded to a halt at the corner of an immense hallway and tested the air with its hairy antennae. The coast was clear so the fidgety little bug scampered ahead, determined to find a meal.

Clean floors made the search for food difficult, and the bug was getting cranky. To make matters worse, it had taken a wrong turn somewhere, and was now in danger of not finding its way back.

Suddenly, the long corridor echoed wildly with the squeaks and squeals of approaching sneakers. The frightened insect released a stinky cloud of gas, then darted for a place to hide. Three giant creatures with spiky heads turned the corner and suddenly filled the hall. The noise they made was deafening as they quickly advanced on the smelly little bug.

In a mad panic now, the bug zipped from side to side, spinning and sliding on the polished floor in a frantic dash for cover. Then just as it lunged for a gap in the base board, a very expensive tennis shoe squished the insect into bug juice with one squeaky step.

"Gotcha!" said Noogy, before he slipped on the mush and almost fell.

Speedy and Bing paid no attention to him and continued their noisy march down the corridor. Dressed in the trendiest teen fashions, they casually lied to each other about their high scores on the latest video games.

"And when the manager saw my score," Speedy said, "he unplugged the game and put in a Love Tester."

"That arcade's gone downhill ever since they took out PacDog Junior," Bing replied.

Noogy scratched behind an ear. "That game gave me fleas."

At the end of the hallway, they passed through a double door flanked by two security guards. The room they entered was enormous; mountains of electronic equipment towered over rows of computer stations. Miles of wire connected video game units to large-screen televisions and desktop monitors. Digital amplifiers sent power pulsing through the entire room in an immense power grid.

Technicians in green radiation suits were busy setting up the day's tests. They fidgeted silently about the room, poking at equipment, jerking on cables and pausing at various stations to check for danger.

"What's with all the geeks?" Bing asked, leaning his skateboard against the wall.

"Must be something special going on today," Noogy replied. "I haven't seen Product Testing this busy since they unveiled Tinkling Tina's Toilet Trainer."

Speedy leaned in close. "I heard the Big Kahuna herself was in on this one."

The three game testers each stole a glance toward the far end of the room where a large two-way mirror looked out over the entire facility. And though they couldn't see anything through the tinted glass, none of them dared look for long.

"Ah, you always say that," Bing said.

"Yeah, quit trying to scare us."

Four scientists in white lab coats fussed around the room making last minute checks on equipment and jotting notes onto clipboards. They wore thick glasses, scratched their heads with number-two pencils, and gave each other quizzical looks.

Speedy, Bing and Noogy lined up at the main play station. Three control units were connected to a stack of wide-screen monitors synced to form one massive gamescreen. A technician in green stood at each game station.

"Hey Sarge, why all the hoopla?" asked Speedy.

The technician ignored him and started attaching sensors to Speedy's chest and forehead.

"You know these techies never talk," Bing said as he worked the kinks out of his neck.

Noogy cracked his knuckles, then slipped his hands into a pair of electronic game gloves wired into the console.

"I've got a good feeling about this game," he said.

After hooking up the three game testers, the technicians silently took their places at various computer stations. They put on green goggles and adjusted headphones and some even inserted tiny nose plugs.

Muttering to themselves, the four scientists in white lab coats gathered around an enormous panel of gauges that monitored the testers' vital signs. The instruments in the panel measured everything from a player's pulse and temperature to brain capacity.

Speedy gave the thumbs-up signal and it began. Lights dimmed and the colors of the game filled the room.

"Good graphics," Bing said.

"Nice interplay," Noogy replied.

"Sweet response time," said Speedy.

Speedy had a habit of chewing on his lip as he played. Bing danced nervously from side to side, using his entire body to move his character. Noogy played with his mouth open and a small pool of saliva formed between his feet.

Being expert gamesters, they advanced through the first few levels with ease. But as the game wore on, the difficulty increased and the three game testers started to sweat.

"Man, those monsters can move," Speedy said.

Needles on some of the panel gauges began to rise as the colors of the game grew darker.

"I'd swear that screen is getting closer," said Noogy.

The technicians showed no emotion, but the four scientists looked worried and shared furtive glances.

"All of a sudden I don't feel so good," Bing said, wiping his forehead.

As the intensity of the game grew to fever pitch, the four scientists kept bumping into each other to get a better look at the panel of gauges. They watched in horror as three needles rose steadily into the red.

Suddenly, one of the game testers screamed.

A strange new creature in the game howled and a burning light blinded everyone in the room. The air snapped and sizzled around them before three sonic booms shook the entire building, knocking scientists and technicians to the ground.

Red lights flashed to the pulse of a raging alarm as people struggled to regain composure. Peering over the panel of gauges, the scientists beheld the vacant row of game stations and the empty game gloves smoldering on the floor. They stared in horror as the large screen flickered back to life and the game resumed with three new characters.

Three new characters that looked exactly like Speedy, Bing and Noogy.

From the two-way mirror halfway up the far wall came a faint stream of laughter.

CHAPTER ONE

Soccer Madness

Penny couldn't hold onto Bailey's face much longer. Her arm was getting tired and Bailey's windmill punches kept getting closer and closer. Penny had managed to keep her younger sister at arm's length by clutching the top of Bailey's head. But all the squirming and wriggling had caused Penny's hand to slip down Bailey's forehead and was now smushing her ten-year-old sister's face. One spin and Penny could lose her grip, and she did not want to come into contact with those tiny fists of fury.

"You give up yet?" Bailey mumbled between Penny's fingers.

Penny really thought today would be different. She woke up in a great mood and had the strange sensation that today would be anything but ordinary. Today, Penny thought, we might actually win.

She looked forward to these Saturday morning soccer games. Penny was actually team captain, but that was only because she was twelve and the tallest. And although she wasn't much of an athlete, Penny didn't mind setting aside her beloved books for this weekly match.

The other twelve-year-old on the team was the school bully, Jack. He wasn't very good at soccer, but he was good at scaring the opponents into making mistakes, opening the way for Marbles to steal the ball. Marbles was eleven and the best player they had. His speed and agility were impressive, but the real reason he was best was because he had the most fun when he played.

Jack's brother, Nick, was the other star of the team. He was in Bailey's class at school and since she didn't concentrate too much on the game, Nick spent most of his time covering for her.

The fight started just after Marbles scored his second goal of the game; three more and the score would be tied. Bailey celebrated the goal with an obnoxious dance directed at the opposing team. The typically friendly members of the other team weren't too happy with that and, after a few whoops and war cries, chased her around the soccer field. Soon, Bailey had both teams in hot pursuit until Penny finally caught up with her and brought the mad scramble to an end.

Bailey refused to repent, so Penny apologized for her. The other team accepted the apology and went back to their positions. Bailey, however, did not accept the apology and promptly head-butted her sister in the stomach. That caught Penny off guard, but she was braced and ready when Bailey charged the second time.

That's when Nick, apparently to show his support for Bailey, ambushed Jack. Jack flipped his younger brother off with a shrug, but Nick was relentless in his attack and soon they were grumbling and growling and wrestling in the dirt.

After awhile, the other team left in disgust.

"You forfeit" Bailey yelled through Penny's hand.

Penny gazed over Bailey at her team. Jack had his brother in a scissor-lock, and flicked the back of Nick's head with his finger.

Marbles was the only one not fighting. His real name was Robert Mirabel, but most people knew him only as Marbles. A size too small for his age, he always seemed to be smiling.

"You guys," Marbles said, bouncing the soccer ball off one knee, "this is getting ridiculous."

"Just 'cause you're older doesn't mean you get to boss me around," Bailey growled, still throwing punches.

"I'm not bossing you around," said Penny. "I'm telling you what to do."

"You're always telling me what to do," Bailey said.

"When are you gonna start listening to me?"

"Never!"

Penny shoved her little sister to the ground then sat on her chest. Her arms ached and she had trouble containing the squirming Bailey.

"See, this is why I don't ask you to play with us, 'cause it always ends up in a big fight."

"Does not," Bailey said.

"Does so. You always take everything so serious. Everyone was having fun except you."

"I was having of fun till you started bossing me around."

Nick stopped thrashing to listen to Penny and Bailey. Jack loosened his grip slightly, but kept an eye on his brother.

"You blame me for everything. It doesn't matter who started it, you always end up blaming me." Bailey wriggled furiously under the weight of her sister.

"That's not true," Penny said, thinking of all the times she blamed Bailey for starting it.

"You never invite me anywhere 'cause you don't want to be seen with me," Bailey said. "You're ashamed of me."

Penny rolled off her sister and sat on the ground.

"Well, maybe if you weren't such a brat all the time."

"You're ashamed of me," Bailey cried. "You don't even want people to know I'm your sister."

Penny didn't know what to say; Bailey was right. She was always reluctant to take her sister along for that very reason. Bailey would find a way to embarrass her or start a fight or do something to ruin the entire day. Sometimes, Penny would even sneak out of the house when Bailey was in the bathroom, so she couldn't tag along.

Nick wriggled free of Jack and helped Bailey to her feet. His face was red and his matted hair held fresh clumps of dirt.

"C'mon, let's get out of here," Nick said.

Bailey screamed at Penny.

"I wish you weren't my sister!"

"Bailey..." Penny didn't know what to say.

Bailey made a rude gesture to Penny then ran off the field. Nick limped after her, hobbled by a painful wedgie.

CHAPTER TWO

Rated D for Dangerous

They stared at the wrinkled paper bag that lay harmlessly on the coffee table. Nick wondered what new delight could be inside the crumpled package. Growing anxious when the mysterious object failed to jump out and announce itself, Nick grabbed the bag with both hands and ripped it open. A thin plastic box slid across the table knocking over a glass of water.

GameMonster, was splashed across the cover in bold letters. Below the title, a gargoyle burst through a television screen.

"A video game," Bailey said. "Looks pretty scary."

"Must be Jack's," Nick said.

"It says it's rated D for dangerous. What's that mean?"

Nick just shrugged.

"Why would Jack buy such a creepy game?"

"Because creeps like creepy things."

Nick inserted the game disc into the GameBox console and the television screen jumped to life. Puddles of color swirled and twisted into large dripping letters; trumpets blared in a mad symphony as the gargoyle held the title, GameMonster, over his head with an evil leer.

"How do you play this game?" Bailey asked.

"Just like all of 'em, I guess--turn off your brain and turn on your reflexes."

A strange landscape appeared on-screen and bizarre creatures attacked them almost immediately. The game moved fast and was full of hideous beasts and impossible animals. Monsters even attacked other monsters while unsightly scavengers crawled out of the shadows to prey on the fallen.

"This game is pretty gory," Bailey said.

"Yeah, but intense," said Nick. "I can't stop playing."

Their characters ran and jumped in stiff zigzags, dodging monsters that charged from every corner of the screen. Now and then, a weapon appeared and whoever grabbed it was able to slay the hungry beasts. If the creatures were not slain fast enough, the weapon morphed into bait that just attracted more monsters.

"There sure is a lot of blood," Bailey said.

"More blood means more points."

"Creepy."

The TV glowed brighter and the shadows of the room darkened as Bailey and Nick ventured further into the game.

"I feel weird," Nick said, "like I'm made out of baloney or something."

Occasionally they found a hiding place, a small safe-zone that creatures couldn't enter. Nick was hiding his man in one of these sanctuaries when Bailey's character tried to enter, but the refuge held only one at a time.

Monsters circled as Bailey searched for another hiding spot. She tried to run but the creatures drew the circle tighter. Nick could only watch as the crowd swarmed in upon his friend. Suddenly a strange new beast broke through the horde of monsters and grabbed her with its sharp claws.

Bailey screamed.

A powerful light blinded Nick, so he never saw the glittering trail of a million molecules flowing into the TV screen. After blinking a few times, his vision returned. Slowly, he turned his head. Bailey was gone.

Shadows danced around the room. On the TV, a huge mouth licked its lips and grinned. The mouth faded and the game resumed with Bailey's character already in a mad dash across the screen. Except it wasn't Bailey's character anymore--it looked more like Bailey herself.

Nick stared at the TV and realized that what was once a standard game character, was now a miniature Bailey. Her joystick sat motionless on the floor, but somehow she was up on the screen dodging monsters.

His hands shook. He dared not look away from the game, but his mind kept returning to the empty space beside him. It was getting hard to think with his baloney brain, but he was pretty sure the game just ate Bailey.

Something told Nick to keep playing. Everything would be all right as long as he kept playing the game, as long as he kept scoring points.

He lunged and dodged and ran across the screen. He flew around the charging monsters with skill and agility, settling into a rhythm that made him feel like he'd been playing this game his entire life. He felt unstoppable as his score kept rising higher and higher.

Suddenly, Bailey stumbled into a trap with another mob of creatures closing in on her. Nick evaded an attack by four flying monsters and bolted around them to protect Bailey. The screen pulsed with the beat of the game and the shadows of the room crept closer. One more leap and he was there, if Bailey could just hang on.

Then a huge claw came out of nowhere and slashed his character across the chest. Nick let out a faint gasp and melted into the TV screen.

A mouth dripping blood licked its lips and burped.

As the evil grin faded, the game resumed with Nick and Bailey--dazed and digitized--leaping and dodging and running for their lives.

CHAPTER THREE

Play at Your Own Risk

Jack stormed into the house like he always did, slamming the door open and announcing his presence. He tossed his backpack on the floor. Marbles caught the door as it bounced back and followed him in.

Penny entered a bit more cautiously. A strange air hung about the place and she had a feeling something was wrong. On their way back from the field, they had seen a bright burst of light come from inside the house--a blue pulsing light Penny had never witnessed before. Standing in the doorway, a weird uneasiness crept over her. Her pulse raced and her mouth went dry.

Marbles walked silently through the house with a puzzled look on his face, his head cocked to one side. Jack didn't seem to notice anything unusual, but that was no surprise. Nick once painted his brother's bedroom door bright pink. It was three days before Jack noticed.

"Nick! What are you up to?" Jack hollered, stomping through the house. "You guys better not be in my room."

"They were in here." Marbles' voice came from the family room. "The TV's still on."

Penny surveyed the familiar room. They'd spilled a glass of water and left the television on, but for Bailey and Nick that was pretty good. Yet, Penny couldn't shake the eerie feeling that something had happened.

"Their video game's still going," Marbles said, pointing to the TV.

"Hey, that's not their video game," Jack yelled. "That's my video game!"

Marbles picked up a joystick and started to play. Suddenly, his mouth fell open and the joystick hit the floor.

"Marbles, what is it?" Penny asked.

His mouth moved but no sound came out.

Penny looked up at the screen but couldn't really tell what she was looking at. She wasn't familiar with this game. To her it was just one big mess of swirling colors and silly creatures. This one looked exactly like every other video game, with spooky landscapes and ridiculous weapons and scared running things. Although in this game, two of the scared running things did look kind of like--

"Bailey and Nick?"

Penny's stomach jumped into her throat and a wave of dizziness washed over her. She moved closer to the TV for a better look.

"Oh my God, they're in the game!"

"That's impossible," Marbles said.

Penny could only nod her head; of course it was impossible. Nobody could be inside a video game--could they?

"How'd they get in there?" Jack asked.

"It's not even a widescreen," said Marbles.

Penny couldn't believe her eyes, only Bailey could manage to get herself stuck inside a video game. And not just any video game, but one of Jack's creepy nasty bloody video games.

"I just bought that game," Jack whined. "I never said they could play it."

"Uh, we should probably do something," Marbles said. "They don't look too happy in there."

"And I sure as heck never said they could be in it," Jack added.

Bailey and Nick ran frantically from one end of the screen to the other, hounded on all sides by strange creatures.

"That's the craziest game I ever saw," said Marbles.

"Man, I hate it when Nick uses my stuff without asking."

"This is too weird," Marbles said.

Penny was dumbfounded, befuddled and thoroughly flabbergasted. She hated video games. They gave her a headache and made her wrists sore. She didn't agree with her teacher, Mrs. Gardner, who went on a tirade every month about how video games promoted mindless violence. But Penny couldn't understand what was so fascinating about killing mutants or running over pedestrians; she would much rather read a good book. She considered these games a big waste of time, and that's not just because she was terrible at them, either.

"How do you think they got in there?" Marbles asked.

"I don't know," Penny said. "Bailey's always going where she's not supposed to, but this is ridiculous."

"I think I have a plan." Marbles picked up the joystick again and started playing the game.

Immediately, a third character appeared onscreen and the game glowed red. Marbles' eyes glassed over and he spoke in a thick sleepy manner.

"If I can just...click on Bailey...maybe I can get her out of there..."

"Yeh, get 'em outa there," Jack said. "I never said they could be in there."

"...and she's worth fifty points. So I'll have Bailey..."

"Marbles, put the joystick down," Penny said.

"...and I could sure use the fifty points."

Penny knocked the joystick out of his hands, then grabbed Marbles by the shoulders and gave him a good shake.

"Snap out of it!"

"Hey!" Marbles shot Penny a dirty look.

"Don't you see? It almost had you, too," Penny said.

Marbles clutched his head in pain as the third character in the game vanished.

"What the heck is going on?" Jack yelled, pounding on the couch.

"Oh man, what happened?" Marbles asked.

"Somehow, that game possesses whoever plays it," Penny said. "It was about to pull you in, too."

"That's a heck of a defect," Marbles said, shaking off his headache.

"I knew it!" Jack said. "Nick's always breaking my stuff before I get a chance to use it." He pounded the couch a few more times.

They stared at the television. Fantastic creatures flew across the screen, chasing Bailey and Nick. Penny reached down slowly and, with a lump in her throat, ejected the disc. The television screen went blue--a terrible, silent blue.

CHAPTER FOUR

Caveat Emptor

The little bells that stores have installed above their doors usually jingle pleasantly when someone enters. This alerts anyone working in the back of the store that they have a customer. When Jack kicked open the front door to Everything Video Incorporated Limited, the cute little bell above the entrance screamed like a spastic monkey.

After an awkward moment, the little bell stopped shrieking and people went back to what they were doing. The manager stood behind the counter talking to a customer while a clerk halfheartedly stocked shelves. A young girl browsed through the used-video bins with her mother.

The three friends got in line behind the man at the counter. Jack and Marbles kept pushing each other out of line while Penny fidgeted anxiously.

"Mr. Traven," the manager said, "this disc is not defective."

"Nothing happens when I win," said Mr. Traven. He wore a blue windbreaker and had little tufts of grey hair growing out of his ears.

"I explained this to you very clearly when you bought the game," replied the manager. "Video poker does not dispense cash."

Mr. Traven pounded the counter. "Then how can they call it poker?" He waved the game case in the manager's face.

"Because that's what it is, Mr. Traven," the manager said, pushing the game aside. "Now, if you'll please let me get back to work--"

"Bah! Go back to work, ya bureaucrat."

The little bell let out a hollow clunk as Mr. Traven shuffled out of the store. Penny, Jack and Marbles stepped up to the counter.

"And what can I do for you kids?"

"We have a problem with one of your games," Penny said.

"Impossible."

"Oh, it's possible," Jack said, pounding the counter like Mr. Traven.

The manager ignored Jack.

"All of our games are guaranteed," he said.

"What does that mean?" Penny asked.

"That means all the games we sell come standard with a limited warranty, factory-inspected seal-of-approval, two discount coupons and a nonessential disclaimer."

"What does that mean...to us?" Marbles asked.

"That means, young Sherlock, there's no way you could be having a problem with one of our games, unless--say, which game were you having a problem with, anyway?"

"GameMonster," Jack said. "Ya bureaucrat."

"Oh." The manager's tone changed. "Look, we can't be responsible for every game we sell. It says right on the box, 'parental discretion advised'."

"So you know what we're talking about," Penny said.

The manager shrugged his shoulders. "No. What are you talking about?"

"You just said--"

"I have an idea. Why don't you kids go on home and try it again. You'll figure it out, just keep playing till you get the hang of it."

The manager dismissed them with a wave of his hand and went back to work rearranging the counter.

"Hey!" Penny said. "This is a matter of life and death. How can you stand there and pretend like you don't know what's going on?"

Penny felt the anger rise. Her parents had always taught her to treat adults with respect but she was losing patience. There was something fishy about all this and the store manager knew more than he was letting on.

"When I bought that game yesterday, there was a salesman in here named Lewis," Jack said. "Where's Lewis?"

The manager froze for an instant, muttered something under his breath, then let out a small sigh.

"Lewis? He's no longer with us--that is--he's not here anymore."

"Well, where is he?" Marbles asked.

"Now listen!" The manager's features darkened. "That salesman's not around anymore and he's not coming back. So my advice to you is to go home and keep playing that game until it sucks you in--er, I mean, until you become one with the--that is, until you can't play it anymore."

The manager's face was twisted and purple, a vein on his forehead throbbed in anger. Penny knew he was about to blow, so she pulled Marbles and Jack away from the counter.

"Uh, you know what, forget it," Jack said.

"Yeah, it's okay. We'll figure it out," Penny said.

"You're not really a bureaucrat," Marbles added.

They crossed the store and stood in a corner wondering what to do next. The manager kept an eye on them as he made a quiet phone call.

The clerk who had been stocking shelves the whole time moved toward the three friends. He was an older man with thick glasses and a hearing aid.

"Psst," the clerk said. "Hey, you kids."

Still feeling wary, they pretended not to hear him.

"You kids best stay away from that game," the clerk said.

That did it. After sharing a surprised look, they scuttled over to the old clerk. They all wanted to speak, but no one knew what to say.

The clerk tapped his hearing aid. "Got this baby turned up to ten. You know someone who played that game?"

Penny, Marbles and Jack nodded in unison.

"And now they're missing?"

"Well," Penny said, "we kinda know where they are."

"They're in that game, ain't they?" the clerk asked.

The three friends nodded in unison again. The clerk looked up to make sure the manager was still on the phone.

"That's what happened to Lewis. He was playing that game and got swallowed up--just like that." The clerk snapped his fingers. "Gone in a flash of light."

"How'd you get him out?" Jack asked.

"I couldn't get him out," the clerk said. "I'm not very good at these games and, well, I accidentally clicked on him."

Penny gasped. Marbles and Jack leaned in closer.

"What happened?"

"He was gone for good," said the clerk.

"How many points was he worth?" Marbles asked.

The clerk looked up in surprise. "Um, two-hundred, I think."

Marbles turned to Penny. "Maybe you're worth more if you're older."

"That game is engineered evil," the clerk said.

"What are we gonna do?" Jack asked.

"My Grandma always said these games were no good," Marbles said.

"Listen," the clerk said, "I know someone who may be able to help, someone who knows about video games."

"Can we trust him?" Penny asked, glancing toward the manager.

"Without a doubt," the clerk said. "We see him in here all the time. Many people consider him to be some sort of video savant."

"Where can we find him?" Jack asked.

"He usually hangs out at that video arcade over on Lane Avenue."

"Thanks, Mister," Marbles said. "By the way, what's his name?"

"Not sure," the old clerk said, "but they all call him Beanie."

CHAPTER FIVE

Level 1

The creature moved as though it didn't see him. It ambled slowly past, and he relaxed for a moment. That's when the ugly beast whirled about and came straight for him. He dove to one side then ran toward the monster's tail like that alligator guy on the Safari Channel.

Nick's head was pounding and he couldn't focus. He was dizzy and scared, his vision completely blurred. Every movement sent little jolts of static electricity throughout his body. He knew that he and Bailey had been pulled into the game somehow, but his muddled brain had not fully accepted this new reality.

Flying monsters filled the sky and all manner of impossible creatures covered the landscape. Nick saw snakebirds and giant wombats, dragonworms, monkeyfish, and even some flying crabs.

The terrain changed constantly, as though it were just another creature in the game. One minute the path was perfectly level, the next it bent skyward and ran up an impossible cliff. Solid earth moved in swift currents while mountains rolled like the ocean. Doorways popped up out of nowhere to release strange animals, then disappeared just as mysteriously.

Bailey was hiding in a safe-zone, one of the small sanctuaries the monsters couldn't penetrate. Unfortunately, these shelters were only temporary and after awhile the sanctuary imploded and any character caught inside was destroyed along with it. The trick was to stay in a safe-zone as long as possible, and then jump out the instant before it blew up.

The monster had Nick on the run. He stopped trying to come up with a plan and just ran for his life. The beast got a little closer with every step. Nick knew it was just a matter of time before the thing caught up and tore him to pieces.

Out of the corner of his eye, Nick saw a flashing blue light. At first, he thought the blinking object was just another creature trying to eat him. But as he got closer to it, he realized the blue flashing thing was a sword.

Nick faked left then dove to the right. The monster bought the fake, giving Nick enough time to grab the weapon and turn to face the beast. Recovering quickly, the creature caught up to him in an instant. Nick sidestepped like a matador and brought the sword down with all his strength.

The beast let out a bloodcurdling cry. The sword disintegrated in Nick's hands as the animal limped off in defeat, its tail flopping helplessly on the ground. But, the wounded monster didn't get very far before it was besieged by a horde of other creatures.

Still dizzy and nauseous, Nick ran to check on Bailey.

She was fine. The school of mud sharks circling her hadn't moved in for the kill yet.

CHAPTER SIX

Beanie and the Digital Mayhem

The J.R.R. Token Arcade was buzzing with activity. The main hall was full and the new Wizard Warp had a line out the door.

The arcade was neutral territory where jocks, nerds, preppies and dweebs all mingled together freely. Seventh-graders crowded around the same games as high-school sophomores. Once inside the arcade, the animosities of the schoolyard were forgotten and the programmed frenzy of digital mayhem ruled.

Jack disappeared as soon as they entered, lost in the electronic uproar. Flashing lights dazzled Penny to distraction as every game buzzed and clanged and chirped it's own symphony of sounds. Marbles saw some kids he knew from school huddled around Speed Reader 5000. They grunted and pointed to the back when he asked if they knew a kid named Beanie.

Penny and Marbles made their way toward the rear of the arcade. Out of the corner of her eye, Penny spotted Jack shoving tokens into a Bionic Butterfly game two rows over.

Penny grabbed Jack by the collar and pulled him off the machine. Two third-graders quickly filled the vacancy.

"Hey, those are my tokens!" Jack yelled. "You brats owe me two dollars!"

The third-graders high-fived each other as Penny and Marbles dragged Jack toward the back of the arcade.

"Hey, what's the big idea," Jack said, wriggling free. "I was just taking a break, you know. That game cost two dollars."

"Look," Penny said. "We need to work together as a team or we'll never figure out how to pull Bailey and Nick out of that game. We can't afford to have you goofing off or getting distracted. If you can't handle it, just say so and Marbles and I will go on without you."

"You two won't get very far without me," Jack replied. "I'm the brains of this outfit."

"Then you'd better come up with a plan real quick, Einstein, or we'll never see Nick and Bailey again."

Jack's face grew red with anger and he stuck his finger in Penny's face. He was about to yell something, but then he took in a long breath and his mouth slowly softened into a smile.

"You owe me two dollars," he said quietly.

Penny was surprised. She expected more of a fight out of Jack. She looked to Marbles for an explanation but he just shrugged his shoulders and smiled. Marbles knew better than to try to explain anything Jack did.

Beanie was in a dark corner of the arcade playing Hell Dorado. Surrounding him was a lumpy group of odd characters studying his every move. Jack and Marbles pushed their way through the gang of disciples. Penny followed in their wake and stood next to Beanie.

"Yer cramping my shooting arm, gorgeous," Beanie said.

"Are you Beanie?" Penny asked.

"The one and only," he replied. "You here for a lesson or just to enjoy the scenery?"

"We'll ask the questions, Romeo," Jack said.

Beanie gestured toward Jack. "I see you brought your muscle with you."

"We were told you could help us with a problem," Penny said.

"That depends," said Beanie. "What kinda problem?"

Penny held up the GameMonster cartridge and a collective gasp came from the gang of onlookers.

"Isn't that game rated I for immature?" someone asked.

"I read that it was banned in four states."

"I heard it did your homework while you played."

Beanie glanced at the game case. Several grimy hands shot out of the crowd and tried to grab it.

"You know anything about this game?" Penny asked, putting the cartridge away.

"GameMonster? Sure, it's the latest from Gargoyle. I was all set to buy one but my old man threw my GameBox out."

"Why'd he do that?" Marbles asked.

Beanie continued playing as he talked.

"I had a marathon session of Beetlemania going and didn't come out of my room for two weeks."

"Wow," Marbles said. "That's gotta be a record."

"What do you know about GameMonster?" Penny asked.

"Not much," Beanie said. "I heard a rumor about some mishap during testing, but that's about it."

Jack elbowed a kid next to him who had gotten too close. "What kind of mishap?"

"I don't know," Beanie said, "something about the point-counter being unstable or the graphics causing brain seizures or something."

"Do you know anyone who's ever played it?" Penny asked.

"Sure, Little Frankie bought one," Beanie said. "But then he ran away from home or something and nobody's seen him since."

"Ran away from home," Marbles repeated.

"And Mongo Tom invited me over to play his, but when I got there no one was home--probably got tired of waiting for me."

"Yeh, got tired of waiting," Jack said.

"And then there's the guy on TV in the gargoyle suit." Beanie looked puzzled. "Hey, what's all this about, anyway?"

"We think we know what happened to your friends," Penny said.

"Get out--you don't think it has anything to do with GameMonster, do you?"

"Don't you find it odd that you've never actually talked to anyone who's played this game?" Penny asked.

"Now that you mention it, yeah, it is kinda odd."

"So will you help us?" asked Marbles.

"Help you do what?" Beanie replied.

"Find out why people are disappearing when they play this game," Penny said.

"We're gonna get to the bottom of this," Jack said. "Are you in or out?"

"Geez," Beanie stammered. "I'm a little busy here, you know. And then I have to fill in for Little Frankie at the Puzzle Port and after that I have my weekly videoholics meeting."

"You do what you want." Penny lowered her voice to a harsh whisper. "But this game destroys people, and everyone who plays it is in danger. So remember that next time one of your friends comes home with one."

"Look, I don't know anything about that," Beanie said. "But if there is something wacky going on, there's only one person I know who could figure it out."

"Well, spill it, Romeo," Jack said.

"There's this crazy old guy," Beanie said. "He's supposed to be some sort of electronics genius."

"Who?" Penny asked.

"His name's Jasper. He lives across town, above the confetti factory."

"Will he help us?" Marbles asked.

"I don't see why not," Beanie said. "The guy's a digital legend--used to design these things."

"Thanks," Penny said.

"No sweat. Hey, what's your name anyway?"

"Her name's Penny," Marbles yelled over his shoulder as he ran to catch up with her.

CHAPTER SEVEN

The Wizard

The confetti factory was in the industrial section of town, on the lower level of one of those monstrous warehouses that take up an entire city block. Dark and dirty, it was the largest beast on a mostly deserted street full of old buildings and abandoned factories. On one corner of the warehouse, next to an alley, was a faded sign that read:

J. KRUMPLING
DIGITRONICS

Rising from the shadows of the alley, a rickety wooden staircase clung to the side of the warehouse and climbed thirty feet up to a lone door. Penny led the way cautiously as the staircase creaked and groaned with every step. Strange noises came from the confetti factory, grinding, crushing blasts that shook the whole building.

Penny was almost to the landing at the top of the stairs when an explosion inside the factory rocked the building. The stairway buckled and threatened to collapse. She jumped the last few steps to the landing.

"You guys okay?"

"I'm alright," Marbles said, getting to his feet.

The explosion inside the factory brought a new machine to life that sent rhythmic pulses through the stairs. Jack scrambled on all fours up the wobbly staircase.

"That was wild!" Jack said, as he reached the landing.

Penny opened the door and stepped cautiously inside. The room was dark, so Penny stopped to let her eyes adjust. Jack and Marbles slammed into her from behind.

"Hey, what'd you stop for?" Jack said.

"I can't see anything," Penny said.

Marbles pushed Jack away from him.

"Quit stepping on me."

"Easy pipsqueak," Jack said.

"Don't call me pipsqueak."

"Quiet," Penny whispered.

They could tell from her tone she wasn't going to put up with any nonsense, so they pushed each other a few times then settled down.

When her eyes finally adjusted to the darkness, Penny followed a narrow path through the dusty boxes and crates that filled the room. The path led to a dark door framed by a sliver of light leaking from the next room. Penny slowly pushed the door open.

An eerie light bathed their astonished faces as they peered into the strange and wondrous room. The illumination was caused by thousands of electronic gadgets and appliances and computers all lit up and working. Every apparatus seemed to be connected and communicating with the thing next to it.

Toasters had digital displays. A lamp gestured wildly with its robotic arms as it conversed with a row of vacuum cleaners. A dishwasher with hundreds of tiny light bulbs was sending love messages in Morse code to the air conditioner. A television argued with a DVD player.

The objects in the room were nothing more than junk, discarded scrap metal, wire, and old appliances. But someone had magically fused them all together and given them intelligence. Someone had brought them all to life.

"Unbelievable," Marbles said.

"I think we're in the right place," Penny said.

Jack tried picking up a stapler but it had roots wired into an old printer. The room buzzed with a vibrant living energy that filled the air and caused Penny to smile for the first time all day.

Just then a door opened, and the collection of gadgets stopped what it was doing to greet the strange man who entered.

A mop of grey hair danced on his head like a poodle trying to jump off a table. He wore a filthy old apron with bulging pockets, and carried a bizarre electronic device. Lost in thought, he muttered to himself as he chewed on a finger.

The living carpet of machinery clicked and bleeped in reverence, trying desperately to grab the old man's attention. Something in the entanglement whistled an alarm and the disheveled scientist finally looked up from his invention.

"Oh, and who have we here?" he asked.

The living circuitry responded with a few blips and bleeps.

"I can see that they're humans, but why are they here?"

Penny couldn't believe it. The crazy old guy was actually communicating with a pile of nuts and bolts. It wouldn't have seemed so strange if the pile of nuts and bolts wasn't talking back to him.

"Um, excuse me. We're looking for Jasper." Penny knew it sounded dumb the moment she said it.

The room erupted in electronic laughter.

"Quiet! Quiet now," the old man said. "Don't mind them; they don't get too many visitors. I'm Jasper, of course, what can I do for you?"

Marbles peered around Penny.

"Were you really talking to this stuff?"

"Of course," Jasper said. The pile of circuits buzzed with scorn at being called stuff. "English translates quite easily into Mechanese."

"We're sorry for bothering you, but we have a serious problem," Penny said.

"Really?" Jasper set his invention down. "What kind of problem? Electronic infection? Digital waste?"

Penny held up the game cartridge.

"Video game."

"That game sucked up my brother!"

"Easy Jack," Penny said.

"Oh, I see. May I?" Jasper took the cartridge from Penny and studied it thoughtfully.

"My friends are trapped inside that game," Marbles said. "Can you help us?"

Jasper shuffled over to the living pile of circuitry. Near an old television, he found a small opening amid the wires and inserted the game disc. The room, which had been quietly clicking and chirping, exploded to life. Lights flashed and motors whirred as every attached gadget pulsed with excitement.

"What do you think?" Penny said. "Can you pull them out of there?"

Jasper emitted a steady stream of mumble as he worked.

"Well, I've plugged the game into IGGI here, and using the Cosmic Problemator program, IGGI's reading the data encoded on the disc, mumble, some sort of helix configuration. I'm not familiar with this code."

"IGGI?" Marbles asked.

"Integrated Gadgets with Genuine Intelligence," Jasper replied. The pile of circuits whistled proudly.

"There they are," Jack said, pointing to the console.

On the dusty old monitor, Nick and Bailey ran for their lives. Jasper tweaked a few knobs and fiddled with some dials.

"Just as I thought, murmur, looks like they've been grafted onto the matrix, some kind of binary molecular transparency."

"That's weird," Marbles said. "It's in the middle of the game. Shouldn't it have started over?"

"Hey yeh, that's not the beginning," Jack said.

"No--yes, mutter, that would make some sort of sense, wouldn't it?" Jasper said.

"What do you mean?" Penny asked.

"Well, mumble, I'm detecting some type of carbon-based encoding that reconfigures the program as the game progresses. It seems to be locked onto the abnormal element with a clear objective."

"The abnormal element?" Penny didn't like the sound of that.

"I thought you said you spoke English," Marbles said.

"Oh yes, sorry," Jasper said. "Apparently, the game will not reset until all available energy is absorbed."

"Meaning Bailey and Nick," Penny said.

"In a manner of speaking."

"This is ridiculous!" Jack said. "Isn't there anything you can do?"

"I can try to pull their moleculars out of the matrix, mumble, but I may do more harm than good."

"Whatever you do, don't hurt them," Penny said.

"Well, that's the real trick, isn't it?" Jasper said. "If I try to rewrite the code without the proper sequence, I could foul up the works for good. And if I try to reprogram the game, they may be deleted."

"They don't look too happy in there," Marbles said.

The screen was a swirl of color and blood and beasts.

"Please hurry," Penny said.

Jasper scratched his head. "Oh, mumble, it's a mutter of a grumble."

CHAPTER SEVEN POINT FIVE

Level 2

Nick's eyes finally adjusted to the kaleidoscopic world of the game. His headache was gone and he could think clearly for the first time since being pulled into GameMonster.

Bailey tried to stick close to him, but had trouble keeping up. She barely escaped an attack by a school of mud sharks; one of them almost pulled her under before Nick drove the creature off. She looked pale and scared, and spent most of her time in the safe-zones.

Nick knew they were on Level 2 because the colors of the game had changed and the monsters moved faster now. His sense of time was distorted so he wasn't sure how long they'd been on this level and he was torn between staying here and advancing through the game. If they stayed on Level 2, they would get used to how fast the monsters moved and maybe have a better chance of survival. On the other hand, if they advanced to higher levels they might find a way out.

Suddenly, Bailey stumbled and fell. A pair of winged dogs bolted toward her. There was no way for Nick to reach her in time; one of the flying dogs was almost upon her. He didn't know what to do. Unable to get up, Bailey was helpless.

Nick leapt without thinking. As he leapt, he reached for his weapon but his hand came up empty. He forgot--he didn't have a weapon. The crimson beast would rip him to pieces when they collided in midair.

But just at the moment of impact a fundamental change came over the dog. With Nick's hands around its throat, the winged canine morphed from a pulsing red to vibrant blue and shifted its momentum. Nick landed near Bailey, but the blue dog spun to attack the other winged creature. The beast had been tamed--it was now protecting them.

Nick helped the fallen girl to her feet and led her away from the battling game-dogs. A sense of calm came over him and he relaxed for the first time since the nightmare began. Colliding with the winged dog restored his confidence.

Nick now realized that being grafted onto the game enlarged his sense of perception, and things that were confusing before, began to make sense. He still felt like himself, but now he was also a part of the game--a digital Nick.

The more he thought about being one with the game, the more his field of vision opened up. Soon the entire horizon shone with a brilliance he'd never noticed before. He recognized that everything in the game-world emanated from a source and flowed through everything else. That source was the game's master program, and being part of that program put him in the path of a constant stream of information.

He practiced tapping into the game-matrix and soon everything came into sharp focus. He could now sense where the danger would come from; it was like being able to see around corners. He had a clear vision of the safe routes to take and the weapons they would need to make it to the higher levels. He was no longer afraid.

Ahead of him, Nick saw the portal to the next level.

CHAPTER SEVEN AGAIN

Computers are Human Too?

"IGGI is having trouble accessing the game's master code," Jasper said, flipping switches and spinning dials.

Penny and Marbles saw Nick's encounter with the game-dogs, and stared anxiously at the screen. Jack paced the floor behind them.

"I need to have Nick home for dinner or my dad's gonna kill me," Jack said.

"I'll try to infiltrate the security system and see if I can break down that code."

Jasper moved to an old keyboard and started entering platform code sequences. The screen blinked a few times then went black.

"Oops," he said.

Penny's stomach did a somersault. "Don't say that!"

Jasper frantically punched in a few codes and the tangle of electronic gadgets screamed as the screen popped back to life.

Jasper worked for hours, all the while mumbling and muttering and scratching his bushy head. Jack and Marbles got restless and situated themselves in various uncomfortable positions between the gadgets and boxes, but Penny never moved from her spot directly in front of the screen. Finally, Jasper's hands dropped slowly to his side and he hung his head.

"I'm sorry kids. I'm afraid there's nothing I can do."

He popped the game disc out of the console and handed it to Penny. IGGI let out a mechanical sigh.

"What do we do now?" Marbles asked.

"I think I may know someone who can help, someone who designs these games."

"Here we go again," Jack said.

"Quiet, Jack." Penny said.

"My old friend Professor Wingnut works for the company that made this game. He may be the only one who can get your friends out of there."

Marbles gave the old scientist a hug. "Thanks for trying, Jasper."

"Where can we find this Professor Wingnut?" Penny asked.

Jasper took a deep breath.

"In the lion's den, where else?"

CHAPTER EIGHT

The Guardians

They followed the highway north through town, past car dealerships and mini-malls. They hurried through the canine quarter, where every yard contained a barking dog that spun into a frenzy when they walked past. Beyond the motel district, the sidewalk ended and the broad avenue became a narrow two-lane highway. Traveling single-file Indian-style along the shoulder of the road, they passed ancient barns and crumbling silos surrounded by construction sites crowded with the skeletons of new houses.

Penny tried not to think about what her parents would do to her if she couldn't get Bailey out of the game. They hit the roof that time Bailey ran away from her at the mall and ended up in the lost and found. Penny spent two weeks in her room for that little stunt. This time they'd probably hit the moon.

Jack amused himself by kicking trash onto the road and punching Marbles in the shoulder every time a truck passed by--in either direction.

The road crossed a broad plain before snaking up into the foothills. Just before the highway turned to skirt a long low ridge, an unmarked road branched off into a valley.

They turned down the road through the wide treeless valley and, after a short walk, came upon a massive wall. Two stainless steel panels formed a gate where the wall crossed the road.

"This must be the place," Penny said, studying the gate.

"Can you see a way through?" Marbles asked.

"Not really. These panels must be four feet thick."

"So is this it, or what?" Jack asked.

"I guess so," Penny replied. "I think this must be the front gate."

"If this is the front gate," Jack said, "then how do we open it?"

Penny tried not to let Jack bother her.

"I don't know, look around."

"I knew we shouldn't have taken this road," Jack said.

"Maybe there's a doorbell or an intercom or something," Marbles suggested.

"Exactly," Penny said. "There's gotta be some way to trigger this gate."

"Maybe we're in the wrong place," Jack said.

Penny took a deep breath. He was beginning to annoy her, but she remained calm.

"I don't think so, Jack. I'm sure this is the place."

"Maybe this is a dead end," Jack said.

"This is definitely not a dead end, we just need to find a way through this gate."

"Maybe this isn't a gate at all, but a big fat dead end and you just don't want to admit it."

Penny let that one get to her. She didn't want to quarrel with Jack, but all his bellyaching was starting to irritate her.

"Why don't you try to come up with a solution for once? All you ever do is complain about everything, and I'm sick of it."

"Well, I'm sick of you!" Jack yelled.

"You want to go home? Turn around and go home, we'll go on without you."

"Who elected you queen? I'm tired of taking orders."

"C'mon you guys," Marbles said.

"We're going in there and we're gonna find that professor," Penny said.

"And how do you plan to do that, yer majesty? There's a stupid wall in the way!" Jack kicked the gate for emphasis.

A gust of wind raised some dust and Penny thought the panel stirred a little.

"Jack, don't--" Penny said.

"A big dumb stupid wall," Jack said, kicking the gate a few more times.

"Stop it!"

Jack kept kicking. Both panels seemed to vibrate slightly.

"Jack, you're gonna get us in..."

Suddenly the ground trembled and both sides of the gate shook violently.

"Trouble," Marbles said, backing away from the gate.

With loud pops and bangs, the two gate panels changed shape, sprouting new sections and expanding skyward until the panels didn't look like panels anymore. In a matter of seconds, the gate had transformed into two towering sentinels of steel.

The steel guardians stood over fifteen feet tall and took up the entire road. Their massive legs pounded the road, slowly at first, then building up to a march. They didn't appear to have any arms, but their blue domed heads contained one large steely eye in the center. The heads swiveled back and forth, as they marched in place.

"This can't be good," said Penny.

"Did I do that?" Jack asked.

Penny stepped toward the guardians. The force of their marching sent thunderous vibrations up her spine.

"Excuse me," Penny said.

A huge, steel foot slammed into the ground inches away from her.

"Excuse me!" Penny yelled.

The marching got faster and shook the earth for miles. Marbles put two fingers in his mouth and blew the loudest whistle Penny had ever heard.

The marching stopped.

Marbles smiled. "That's a little trick my Grandma taught me."

"Knock knock," Penny said, "anybody home?"

One of the enormous steel beings bent over and stuck its huge round eye in Penny's face. The sentinel blinked once.

"We're here to see Professor Wingnut," Penny said.

The steel sentinel straightened up, realigning with its twin. The guardians shook for a moment as though they were sharing information, then a small speaker appeared on the right foot of each sentry. They took turns speaking.

"Invalid password, can't process Wingnut,"

"Admittance denied, this gate remains shut,"

"Error has occurred, please try once again,"

"Must use proper code, must re-enter PIN."

"What the..." Jack said.

"They're robots," said Marbles.

"Rhyming robots," Jack added.

"Well, we'd better come up with the password or we'll never get past these things," Penny said.

"We could pretend we're tourists," Marbles whispered.

Penny shrugged. It was worth a shot.

"Hello? We're on vacation--you know, like tourists--and we were hoping to take a tour of your facility. What do you say?"

"No visitors here, no tourists today,"

"Crowds are a problem, kids get in the way,"

"No entry for you, it's useless to try,"

"Save it for Sony, they might let you by."

A long segmented arm snaked out of the left guardian's side and paused in mid-air. The right guardian produced a similar arm and with a tremendous clang, high-fived its companion.

"Rhyming guards," Jack said. "That's pretty stupid."

"What are we gonna do?" Marbles asked.

"We're gonna think of a way to get past these guys," Penny said.

"I've got an idea," Marbles said. "We can wait until somebody leaves. They'll have to open up to let them out, and that's when we sneak in."

"We could be here all day waiting for someone to leave," Penny replied. "And there's no way to sneak through without being seen."

"Well, if we can't go through," Jack said, "maybe we can go over."

"Jack, no!" Penny yelled.

But it was too late. Jack jumped up onto a gigantic foot and started shimmying up the enormous leg.

"Oh, brother," Marbles said. "He's gonna get himself killed."

"Jack, get down," Penny yelled. "What do you think you're doing?"

"What does it look like I'm doing? I'm getting past these stupid guards."

Jack was about halfway up the leg when the guardian tossed him off with a slight kick. He flew over Penny and Marbles, flailing his arms like a wounded duck, and then landed in a heap on the pavement.

"Are you alright?" Marbles asked.

"I don't know," Jack replied, getting up slowly. "What does a broken butt feel like?"

"Boy, was that a stupid stunt!" Penny said.

Marbles leaned against the guardian on the left and raised himself up on his tiptoes to reach the speaker.

"Uh, visitation authorization...requestation."

Penny rolled her eyes as Marbles backed away from the potentially dangerous foot.

"Verification--complication--violation," the left guardian replied.

"We don't have time for this," Penny said. "It's a matter of life or death!"

"No entry today, so please save your breath," the guardian said.

The steel guardians shook with mechanical laughter, apparently very pleased with themselves, and gave each other another high five.

"How are we gonna get past these guys?" Jack asked.

"Another attempt would not be wise," a guardian replied.

Penny grabbed Marbles and Jack, and silently led them away from the guardians.

"Look," Penny whispered, "we can't afford to waste time with these robots."

"Well, what do you want us to do?" Jack said.

Penny held up the video game cartridge.

"Every minute we're out here, Bailey and Nick are fighting for their lives in this game. We have to figure out a way to get past these guards and in to see the professor."

"You think they're still okay?" Marbles said, pointing to the video game.

"I don't know," Penny said. "But if we can't even get past the gate, we'll never be able to help them."

"Right," Marbles said, and stormed over to the guardians with a dangerous look on his face.

Penny put the game back in her pocket and smiled as Jack limped after Marbles. She had hoped pulling the game out would inspire them, and judging from the way Marbles charged the sentinels, it looked like she was right.

"Okay, metalheads," Marbles shouted. "Let's see if you can find something that rhymes with...purple!"

The guardians stiffened and were silent for a long moment. The right guard, whose turn it appeared to be, shook and trembled and whirled its head from side to side. It emitted a low choking sound as its gears jammed up and ground against one another.

"Alright Marbles!" Jack said.

The guardian's huge head spun completely around, its silver eye blinking rapidly. The left sentinel snaked an arm up and slapped its sputtering partner on the top of its dome. Jabbering a bunch of nonsense, the right guardian tried to pull away from its twin.

"I can't believe that worked," Marbles said.

Penny walked up to the left guardian and spoke into its foot.

"How do you feel about the word...orange?"

The left guardian groaned and from the speaker came a series of mutterings in alphabetical order. The sentinel was rapidly searching for a word to rhyme with orange.

"Bora—cloro—door—four—gore--"

"Marbles you're a genius," Penny said. "Not being able to rhyme somehow jams up their gears and sends them into a tailspin."

Just then, one of the snake-like arms reached down and scooped Penny off the ground. The guardian held her in front of its unblinking mechanical eye.

"Penny!" Jack cried.

"Give it another word!" Marbles yelled.

The steel hand tightened its grip, slowly crushing her. Out of breath and losing consciousness, Penny couldn't even think of another word, let alone say one.

Marbles ran up to the guardian's foot and yelled into the speaker.

"Silver! Silver! Silver!"

The guardian shook uncontrollably as smoke rose from its spinning head. The giant metal hand opened and Penny landed hard on the pavement next to Marbles.

"You okay?" he asked, kneeling beside her.

Penny coughed and tried to catch her breath.

"I'll be all right," she wheezed.

With smoke rings billowing from their heads, the guardians detached from one another with a metallic pop. All four arms now fully extended, they batted each other silly in a giant android slapping match. Sparks flew as metal slammed against metal. All the while, their gears ground away searching for words that rhymed.

"We'd better go," Penny said, getting to her feet.

They ran between the guardians legs, careful to avoid being stepped on by the massive steel feet.

Penny glanced back over her shoulder at the battling sentinels as she ran. She couldn't help wondering, now that they were in, would they be able to get out?

"Rhyming guards," Jack said as he ran. "Pretty stupid."

CHAPTER NINE

Yellow Bifocals and Red Tape

Corporate headquarters was a large dark building of steel and glass that sat at the end of the valley. Situated on a small rise, its sleek lines and sharp angles stood in contrast to the flowing green of the glen.

Near the main entrance, a stainless steel sign read:

GARGOYLE ENTERPRISES

Jack pulled one of the doors open and sauntered in. The monstrous door slammed shut before Penny and Marbles could enter. Marbles opened it again and held it for Penny.

The lobby was extensive. Covered in black marble that reflected no light, it had a high ceiling but no windows. Low corridors lead off into the dark depths of the building. The only furniture in the great hall were four black desks that formed a long row in the middle of the immense floor.

The four desks were occupied by four female receptionists, each dressed in a different shade of pink. They sat typing away on their keyboards, trying to talk over each other.

The first receptionist had her hair in a bun and wore a pair of outdated horn-rimmed glasses.

"My Hubert was given the Junior Scholastic Over-Achiever Award for the second year in a row," she said.

"Well," said the second receptionist, "they really just give those out to the problem kids."

"My Stuart had twenty-six A's on his last report card," said the third receptionist. She typed frantically on her keyboard occasionally lifting her yellow bifocals to inspect her work.

"And you were worried he wouldn't fit in at Clown College," the fourth receptionist replied, filing her nails. She kept her hair long and wore white pearl earrings.

"Well, my Sophie's pig won blue ribbon at the county fair this year," the second receptionist said, piling on another layer of bright red lipstick to her already vibrant lips.

"What ribbon did Sophie win?" asked the first receptionist with the black horn-rimmed glasses.

"Excuse me," Penny said, stepping up to the first desk. "Can you help us?"

The receptionists shifted in their seats and huffed impatiently at the interruption.

"Do you have an appointment?" asked the first receptionist, wriggling a hawkish beak that held up the horn-rimmed glasses.

"Not really," Penny replied. "We need to see Professor Wingnut."

The third receptionist peered over her yellow bifocals. "You can't see anyone without an appointment."

"Look lady, we need to see the professor," Jack said, stepping up. "Where is he?"

The receptionists laughed at this.

"If you don't have an appointment, then you must take a number." Black Horn-rims gestured toward a number dispenser on the edge of her desk.

Penny, Jack and Marbles looked around in bewilderment.

"But there's no one else here," Marbles said.

"You must take a number," Red Lipstick said. "And then wait until your number is called."

Marbles pulled a number from the dispenser.

"Zero zero one."

"I wonder what number they're on now," Jack said.

"We don't have time for this," said Penny.

The receptionists typed furiously, avoiding eye contact with the kids. After a few minutes of strained silence, Black Horn-rims let out a heavy sigh.

"Number one?" Still seated, she craned her neck and made an exaggerated sweep of the room. "Number one?"

Penny, Jack and Marbles rushed up to her desk. Marbles threw the number on her desk.

"Good afternoon," Black Horn-rims said. "What can I do for you?"

"We need to see Professor Wingnut," Penny said.

"Well then, you need to fill out appointment-forms six through nine and release-forms twelve through eighteen," she said, handing Penny a pile of forms. "In triplicate."

"It's urgent," said Jack. "We need to see him right away."

"Urgent? Well, why didn't you say so? In that case, you'll need to fill out urgency-forms forty-two through fifty." She handed Jack the forms.

"This is ridiculous," Marbles said.

Penny and Jack scribbled away frantically, filling out the forms the receptionist gave them. Penny gathered the forms and approached the desk again.

"Good afternoon," Black Horn-rims said. "And what can I do for you?"

"You just gave us these forms to fill out and now we're giving them back to you."

"Did you fill them out?"

"Of course we filled 'em out," Jack yelled, "or we wouldn't be giving 'em back to you!"

"Well, you don't give them to me, silly child, you take them to that desk over there." Black Horn-rims nodded toward the second receptionist who was applying yet another layer of red lipstick.

They marched over to the desk and waited impatiently until the receptionist finished coating her lips.

"We were told to give these to you." Penny said.

Red Lipstick yanked the forms out of Penny's hands. Her face was pale and sweaty and she made low grunting noises as she studied the paperwork. Abruptly, she stopped.

"Oh dear, tsk tsk tsk." Red Lipstick clucked a few times then tossed the forms onto her desk. With a wave of one hand, she dismissed the kids as the other hand reached for the lipstick case.

"What's the problem?" asked Penny

"Well, you didn't fill out your paperwork properly. You must start over."

"Wait a minute," Jack said. "What's wrong with it?"

"You forgot to dot this 'i' right here," she said, pointing to the paper. "Start over."

"You're nuts, lady. We dotted that 'i'," Jack said.

"Gimme that!" Marbles grabbed the form off the table, drew an elaborate dot on the offending 'i', then slammed the form back down on the desk.

Red Lipstick grunted and snorted as she looked the form over.

"Okay. You're all set," she said, "except for one thing."

"I know I'm going to regret this," Penny said. "But what would that be?"

"You never filled out requisition-form thirty-six. You can't go anywhere without requisition-form thirty-six."

"So, let's have it," Jack said.

"Oh, I don't have that particular form here at my desk. You have to get it at that desk over there." Red Lipstick pointed to the third receptionist. "Only she can't give it to you until she signs off on these."

"Then let us take these forms to her so she can sign off on them and we'll bring you back requisition-form thirty-six," Penny said.

"Oh, I can't let you have these forms until you've filled out that one," Red Lipstick replied. "That is very explicit in the receptionist's manual."

"You have a manual for this?" Marbles asked. "I wonder who wrote that thing."

Penny stared blankly at Jack and Marbles; she wasn't sure what to do. She thought all they had to do was get inside corporate headquarters and they'd be home free. Now it looked like they'd never get past these silly receptionists.

Suddenly, Jack got a very curious look on his face.

"We, uh," Jack leaned toward Red Lipstick, "we just talked to that other receptionist and she was all out of that particular form. She was hoping you had an extra copy you could give to us."

"Well isn't that just typical? She's always borrowing things from me." Red Lipstick snorted as she handed Jack the form.

The third receptionist chewed on the end of her yellow bifocals and wrinkled her face in a fake smile as Penny handed her the pile of forms.

"These are the forms you need," Penny said, "all filled out, no mistakes, in triplicate."

The receptionist never stopped chewing as she pulled the yellow bifocals out of her mouth and immediately inserted a pencil. With the bifocals bouncing on the end of her nose, she looked over the forms.

"Yep, it's all there," Marbles added, "in triplicate."

"Well, it seems you've made a serious mistake. You filled out release-form thirteen, twice. And that just won't do."

"We were told to do that by the first receptionist," Jack said.

"You were?" Yellow Bifocals stared at Jack. "Now why would she tell you to do a thing like that?"

"Because she said you were always goofing up and losing papers," Jack answered.

"She said that? Well, of all the nerve! I'm not the one always goofing up, she is. Why just the other day she signed acquisition-form ninety-nine instead of stamping it."

Jack leaned in close. "And she also said you're the reason the reception area smells funny."

"She said what?" Yellow Bifocals spit out the pencil; little yellow flecks of pencil paint remained stuck to her lips. Her cheeks turned red and her face puffed up as she slammed her stamp down onto the pile of forms, page after page. "That's the last time I drive her kids to soccer practice!"

Penny gathered up the papers again and took them over to the last receptionist. She was younger than the others, and wore a white pearl necklace.

"We were told to bring these forms to you," Penny said, handing her the pile.

"That's right," she said, filing her nails. "No one goes anywhere without my stamp."

"Well, actually," Jack said, "that receptionist over there, said this was just a formality and that you needed to feel important."

White Pearls froze.

"She said what now?"

Penny felt her stomach do a flip and then a couple of somersaults. Marbles stared at Jack.

"Well, she said that your rubber stamp didn't really mean anything," Jack said.

Penny's vision darkened and little spots of light danced in her head. They were almost through, why was Jack antagonizing them now? Penny could barely hear what was being said. She tried to tell Jack to stifle it, but the air had gotten very thick and cloudy all of a sudden.

"You wouldn't be pulling my leg now, would you?" White Pearls asked.

"Oh, no ma'am," Jack said. "She was very insistent that you were the weak link in this chain."

"Well, I'll show her whose stamp carries the most ink." White Pearls stood up. "You kids are just going to have to start all over."

That snapped Penny out of it.

"What?"

White Pearls stormed over to Red Lipstick's desk and threw the tattered pile of papers at her.

"Hey! What's the big idea?" Red lipstick said.

"So, my stamp doesn't mean anything, eh?"

"What in the world are you talking about?"

White Pearls grabbed all the papers on Red Lipstick's desk and threw them up in the air.

"Keep it down you two," Black Horn-rims said. "Get back to work."

"Oh, quit your squawking," Yellow Bifocals said. "You're always trying to boss us around."

Black Horn-rims got up and stood over Yellow Bifocals.

"Excuse me?" Black Horn-rims said. "I am the main receptionist here and you need to start listening to me."

"I'll start listening to you when you start making sense," Yellow Bifocals said.

"I've got more sense in my delete key than you have in your whole keyboard," Black Horn-rims said.

"Well, at least I can type more than four words a minute," Yellow Bifocals said.

"How would we know?" Black Horn-rims replied. "You never do any work."

White Pearls was still yelling at Red Lipstick.

"And that perfume you wear smells like carpet cleaner."

"At least I didn't get my driver's license from a Cracker Jack box," Red Lipstick replied.

"That ought to hold them for awhile," Jack said.

As the receptionists threw papers and screeched at each other, Penny led her friends into one of the low corridors leading off the lobby and the three of them followed it into the depths of corporate headquarters.

CHAPTER TEN

Level 3

The third level of the game opened up before him as he stepped off the portal platform.

Strange blue obelisks grew in scattered clusters like plants rising out of the silver landscape. Dark fortresses loomed in the distance through a thick orange haze.

Nick took a deep breath then reached for Bailey's hand-- nothing. That's funny, he thought, she was there just a minute ago.

He turned to find Bailey clinging to the portal, shaking in terror. Nick grabbed the frightened girl and quickly yanked her off the platform just seconds before it exploded.

The disturbance attracted a gang of beasts and Bailey and Nick were once again on the run.

But this time Nick ran with confidence. His expanded awareness enabled him to tap into the game's matrix and follow a visible trail through the mayhem. Instead of feeling like an outsider in an alien world, he flowed across familiar terrain with ease.

Third level creatures moved with terrifying speed. Larger and meaner, they appeared to be a sinister mixture of the worst beasts from other levels.

A cloud of buzzing insects emerged out of nowhere and swarmed around Bailey and Nick. Swatting at the thick horde was useless; the swarm moved in unison as though it were one entity. It attacked, however, as a thousand different animals.

Nick felt dozens of painful stings as he tried desperately to fend off the attacks. He managed to hit a few of the pesky bugs and even caught one. Opening his hand slowly, he saw for the first time what was stinging him. It was a tiny winged elephant with sharp tusks.

Nick dropped the elephantbug in horror and reached for Bailey. She was curled up in a ball, her arms shielding her head. Nick picked her up and ran toward a small lake just over the hill.

He plunged into the lake with Bailey in his arms, hoping to escape the swarming elephantbugs. The horde hovered at the edge of the lake but did not attack. Nick relaxed as Bailey washed herself in the cool water. The lake felt wonderful after the awful stings and Nick swam like he was in his neighborhood pool back home.

But this was not his neighborhood pool. And he was nowhere near home.

In an instant, the water turned icy cold, shocking the two swimmers. Suddenly, Nick couldn't move his arms or legs. He was a popsicle. The lake had frozen over and was now a solid sheet except for two surprised heads poking up out of the ice.

Her eyes practically popping out of her skull, Bailey looked to Nick for help. He could do nothing, and was upset with himself for letting his guard down and getting Bailey frozen like this. All he could manage was to stare helplessly at his friend.

Then Bailey smiled for the first time since being pulled into the game. Frozen like a popsicle, she smiled at Nick.

And then she peed.

CHAPTER ELEVEN

Chapter Evelyn

Goyle paced in front of the large steel desk and tried to control his nerves. It was no use, his left ear kept twitching with spasms and his tail spun in circles. These meetings with the corporate president always made him nervous.

Evelyn Erickson sat behind the desk, punching numbers into a computer. She wore a leopard-skin suit, quite possibly made from a real leopard, and a pair of reading glasses that perched impatiently on the end of her nose.

"Sales are up, Goyle," Evelyn said. "I told you GameMonster would be a hit."

"Yeah, boss. You were right about that, boss," Goyle said.

"I don't care what those crazy scientists in the lab think, it's the rhino horns and elephant ears that make this whole thing work."

"Yeah, boss."

Evelyn looked up from her work.

"Oh for cryin' out loud, Goyle, you're twitching again."

Goyle grabbed his ear with one hand and tried to hold his flopping tail with the other.

"Goyle, if I've told you once I've told you a thousand times, stay away from the candy machines."

Goyle looked embarrassed.

"I know you've been down on the lower levels camped out in front of those vending machines," she said. "You've probably been down there all morning stuffing your face with Chocolate Plops and Chewy Worms."

Goyle's tail flipped back and forth ferociously.

"Don't you know what that stuff does to concrete?"

Goyle shook his head and looked away.

"You're a gargoyle. You're made out of cement! That stuff is going to rot your insides out."

Goyle scratched his head nervously and stared at the ceiling.

"And all that junk's giving you the jitters."

Goyle danced in a little circle trying to step on his agitated tail, but the tail wisely avoided his heavy feet.

Evelyn shook her head in disgust and went back to her numbers.

"Yeh, boss, but...hey boss?" Goyle said, standing still for a second.

"Yes? What is it now?"

"What if we run out of rhino horns and elephant ears?"

"It doesn't matter, you thick-headed gargoyle, do you have any idea how big an elephant ear is? We can make a thousand games from just one elephant ear and a little rhino dust."

"Oh yeah, I guess elephants are pretty big, huh boss Otherwise, they couldn't call them elephants."

Evelyn rolled her eyes in disgust.

"And pretty soon," Goyle continued, "every kid is gonna wanna play GameMonster, huh boss?"

"Money in the bank, Goyle. Money in the bank."

"Yeah, money in the bank," Goyle said. "Money in the bank and kids in the game."

He stopped pacing and tugged nervously at his ear.

"Stop that!" Evelyn commanded.

Goyle dropped his hand to his side and absent-mindedly scratched his leg.

"Hey boss, tell me again why we need the kids in the game."

"Goyle, we've been through this a hundred times." Evelyn logged off her computer, walked over to the bar and poured herself a drink. "When is it going to get through that concrete skull of yours?"

"One more time, boss." Goyle pulled on his tail anxiously. "I'll remember this time, I promise. Just tell me one more time."

"Oh, alright," Evelyn said, slurping her drink. "Kids get sucked into GameMonster for one very simple reason--I hate kids! Well, that and I want to take over the world."

"The whole world?"

Evelyn paced the room as she spoke.

"In my rabid quest to build the largest video-game company in the world, I stumbled upon a secret. A delightfully wicked secret that will make our mainframe computer the most powerful computer on the planet."

"The whole planet?"

"We found a way to activate a child's bloodlust by increasing the violence in video games. When children are racking up points in GameMonster, their evil gene is activated and they become bloodthirsty. GameMonster senses this through the genes of endangered species, then locks onto that child and sucks them right in." Evelyn smiled with giddy pleasure then inhaled the rest of her drink.

"Not just kids either, huh boss?"

"That's right, Goyle. The beauty of GameMonster is that anyone who plays it will eventually be grafted onto the matrix. Our mainframe computer then absorbs their life force. Children have higher levels of energy than adults, and that energy is what we need to make ours the most powerful computer in the world."

"The whole world."

"So, you think you can remember that, mortarhead?" Evelyn poured herself another drink. "I always feel a little clichéd explaining the master plan."

"Yeah boss, I can remember," Goyle said. "Evil is, as evil does."

Evelyn rolled her eyes. "Close enough."

A red light on the control panel of the large steel desk started blinking.

"Hey boss, the front-gate alarm is going off!"

"Those dunderheads must be off their rockers again. It never fails--as soon as the warranty expires, they always fall apart."

Evelyn sat down at the desk. "I wonder if this has anything to do with those pesky kids that store manager called to warn me about. Better check it out, Goyle."

"You got it, boss. I'll check it out." Goyle smiled as he headed for the door.

"And stay away from those candy machines," Evelyn said.

That last order hit Goyle on the back of the head like a wet towel. His smile disappeared as he slouched out of the room.

CHAPTER TWELVE

Pixel Dust and Digital Soup

Corporate headquarters was a maze of hallways and corridors. Each new section they came upon looked exactly like the last--walls, ceilings and floors were all painted Acme white. Every door was closed and locked, with no name or number on it. There were two elevators near a stairwell, but there were no buttons to call the elevators. They found the stairwell doors unlocked, however, so the kids went up to the next level.

Penny saw a shadowy figure at the end of the corridor turn a corner and disappear.

"Someone's down there," Penny said.

Jack and Marbles practically ran her over trying to get to the end of the hall.

Penny hurried after them and turned the corner just in time to see a man in a long white coat at the far end of the hallway disappear around another corner.

They raced after him, turning corner after corner as he wound his way through the maze of corridors. At the end of a particularly long hallway, the man opened an unmarked door and entered the room.

Jack bolted down the hall as the door slowly closed. Diving headfirst he slid across the floor and managed to wedge his hand in the door just before it shut.

"Alright Jack," Marbles whispered.

Penny and Marbles helped Jack to his feet, and this time he held the door open for them.

The room was a maze of tables, each one home to a different experiment. Huge arrays of bubbling beakers overflowed with strange fluids; Bunsen burners heated chemicals to the boiling point, forcing the frothy liquids to spill over into other beakers down the line, each time changing colors. Franklin Towers shot sparks of lightning from one table to another. One entire shelf along a wall held perpetual-motion machines, while above, a complex mobile of spinning magnets hung from the ceiling, rotating and revolving with no visible connections. A cardboard box on the floor held an assortment of squirming robotic appendages, and off in a dusty corner, a white rat raced away inside a rusty metal wheel.

Busy with their experiments, the scientists never noticed the kids enter the laboratory. They wore white lab coats and talked to each other as they worked.

One of the scientists had wild grey hair and a balloon nose that held up thick glasses.

"Hey Sparks, how's that Posterior Motivator coming along?"

"Are you still tailing behind on that one?" asked a short scientist with a chunky bald head.

"I'm having trouble with my Gluteus Maximator," Sparks replied. Tall and thin with black hair, he stared at his experiment in confusion.

"Wingnut," the bald scientist said, "can you please get your pixel dust out of my radio-carbon? It's jamming the signal."

Penny's heart skipped a beat when she heard the name Wingnut. Finally, after all they'd been through, they found Professor Wingnut."

"That's not my pixel dust, Beaker," the grey-haired scientist said. "I think it's Bunsen's."

"I gave mine to Sparks for that digital soup," Bunsen said. She was the only female scientist of the group and she hummed softly while she worked.

"What a disappointment that was," Sparks said. "Nobody liked my cream of electricity."

"Well, you shouldn't have given us metal spoons," Beaker said.

"Ha!" Jack slapped his hand over his mouth trying to contain the laughter, but it was too late. The damage was done.

Test tubes crashed to the floor. Experiments exploded. A Petri dish flew across the room. Someone screamed.

"How'd they get in here?" Beaker asked.

"They're not sterile!"

"Somebody call security," Bunsen said. Green slime oozed down the front of her lab coat.

"They're probably crawling with microbes and particulates and bacterium," Sparks said from under a table.

"I guess they're not used to visitors," Marbles said.

"Who are you and what do you want?"

"We're looking for Professor Wingnut," Penny said.

"Why? Who sent you?" Wingnut asked, picking up the pieces of his dropped experiment.

"Some old dingbat named Jasper," Jack said.

"Jasper, you say?" Wingnut pulled his gloves off and walked over to them. "Jasper Krumpling? Why, I haven't seen that quack in ages. How is old Jasper, anyway?"

Marbles shrugged. "A few floats shy of a parade."

"Two rings short of a circus," Penny added.

Jack tried to add his own clever remark, but when nothing came out, he just bit his lip and stared at the ground. "He's fine."

"Sounds like Jasper," Wingnut said, as the other scientists gathered around. "So, what can I do for you kids?"

"We've got kind of a problem with one of your products," Marbles said.

Beaker scratched his bald head. "The Hindenburg Action Set?"

Sparks leaned forward. "Captain Combat's Easy-Cook Oven?"

"Tinkling Tina?" Bunsen asked.

Marbles rolled his eyes. "One of your video games."

"There's only one video game that would bring you kids here," Wingnut said.

"GameMonster," said Penny, holding up the game cartridge.

All four scientists gasped in horror.

"That game sucked up my brother!" Jack cried.

"I knew that game would come back to haunt us," Sparks said.

"It's not our fault," said Beaker. "We told them what would happen if they used our experiments in a video game."

Bunsen shook her head sadly. "We tried to warn them, but they just smiled and told us to get back to work."

"It was those awful programmers," Wingnut said. "They took our research and engineered this game to be evil."

"That thing needs to be destroyed," Sparks said.

"No!" Penny clenched the game cartridge. She didn't make it this far just to have some wacky scientist ruin everything.

Marbles tugged softly on Wingnut's lab coat.

"Professor," he said, "my friends are trapped inside that game. We need your help."

Wingnut scratched his head as he gazed down at Marbles.

"If old Jasper had confidence in me, then I've got to give it my best shot. Let's have that game."

Penny hesitated, but deep down she knew she had no choice but to trust this crazy clown scientist and his nutty cohorts.

"Please be careful," she said, handing Wingnut the game.

The scientists gathered around an enormous contraption that took up one entire wall of the laboratory. It was some sort of electronic console covered with all sorts of levers and dials and gauges. In the center of the console was a large video screen, and below that several ancient joysticks lay covered in dust.

"Don't worry kids, Wingnut's on the case." He smiled as he inserted the game disc into the machine.

Suddenly, an alarm sounded from inside the machine and the entire apparatus started to shake. Dials spun and levers flip-flopped back and forth. A panel shook off and crashed to the ground. Bunsen quickly punched in a code on one of the keyboards attached to the console and the alarm stopped.

"You forgot the security code," Bunsen said.

"Oh yes," said Wingnut. "Quite right." He went to work inputting data on a keyboard and the game began.

The screen erupted in a blaze of color and motion. Dark figures and shadowy shapes flew across the screen at every angle. In the middle of it all, Nick and Bailey ran for their lives.

"I can't help feeling somewhat responsible for what's happened to those poor kids," Wingnut said. "After all, it was our research that helped create this game."

"Our research was meant to help mankind," Bunsen said, "not throw harmless children into violent video games."

"That's right," said Wingnut. "Just before GameMonster was ready for testing, the master programmers snuck in their own secret codes, attaching malicious programs to files already in place. When I discovered what was going on, I did some secret programming of my own."

"Wingnut," Beaker said. "You old rapscallion."

"What did you do?" Marbles asked.

"I put in a safeguard," Wingnut replied.

"A what?" asked Jack.

"A sanctuary," Wingnut said. "A portal in the game where a character's code is unlocked and can then be downloaded back to the real world," Wingnut said.

"A wormhole," Sparks said.

"A trap door," said Bunsen.

"An escape hatch," Beaker added.

Jack and Marbles looked at each other in confusion.

"A hidden exit!" Penny cried.

"Exactly," Wingnut said. "And I seem to remember installing the first hidden exit on the second level."

Marbles gazed up at the screen. "But they're already on the third level."

"Not to worry," Wingnut said. "There is another portal on the fourth level, only it's much more difficult to reach."

"I thought you said not to worry," Marbles replied.

"Well, from the looks of things they're not even gonna make it to the fourth level," Jack said.

"Their only hope is to advance to the next level and somehow find that door," Wingnut said.

"They'll never find it," Sparks said.

"The odds are too great," Bunsen added.

"What if someone were to lead them?" Penny asked.

One by one, the scientists turned and stared at Penny.

"But that would mean..."

"You'd have to..."

"go into the game..."

"Absolutely not," Wingnut said. "It's far too dangerous. They'll just have to find it on their own."

"I can't take that chance," Penny said, picking up a joystick. "I have to try and save my sister."

Marbles grabbed Penny by the arm. "But you're terrible at video games. You even said so yourself."

"Don't do it, child," Wingnut said.

"I don't have a choice," she replied.

Suddenly, Penny felt a strong hand on her shoulder.

"My turn."

"No," Penny said to Jack. "I need you to stay here in case I don't make it."

"You won't make it." Jack took the joystick from her. "You stink at video games. I'm the best player we've got."

The scientists hesitated for a split second, then went to work on Jack. Sparks attached sensors to his forehead as Bunsen took his pulse. Beaker scribbled the data on a notepad.

"Jack, yer crazy," Marbles said.

"Maybe," said Jack, "but I'm going in anyway. Now, where's that drain, Doc?"

"Portal," Wingnut said. "On the fourth level, once you get beyond the flying hills, you'll run into a thunderstorm. You must catch the blue lightning for the door to appear."

"What will this door look like?" Jack asked.

"It'll look like an outhouse."

"A what?" said Jack.

The other scientists laughed.

"What's an outhouse?" Marbles asked.

"Back when Wingnut was a pup, that's what folks used for a bathroom," Sparks said.

"That's the sanctuary," Wingnut said. "You must get everyone inside."

Jack was already lost in concentration. His breathing grew heavy and his eyes closed to a squint.

"And remember," Wingnut said, "stay away from the gargoyle."

The pace of the game quickened as Jack's reflexes slowed down. It wasn't long before he stumbled.

"Jack, be careful," Penny said.

But he had already made his mistake and the new beast emerged with a roar. Jack dissolved into the game in a trail of color. Just before he disappeared, Penny could've sworn he smiled.

Jack landed with a plop. Unfortunately, it was onto the back of a snarling two-headed garbage eater.

CHAPTER THIRTEEN

Level 4

Nick's brain blinked.

The game world paused and time skipped a beat as the very fabric of the game was ripped open. Lightning flashed in the distance and a dark object dropped from the sky.

Grabbing Bailey, Nick ran toward the recent arrival. He knew immediately it was another person from the outside world entering the game. Some of the creatures noticed the new presence also and created a small stampede in that direction.

Nick followed the digital trail until it led him to a lone garbage eater. These grey drooping beasts usually hung out in the shadows, scrounging for tidbits and leftovers. They rarely attacked, but could be dangerous when cornered.

The hairy monster sat on its haunches, lazily swatting at something on its back. Unable to knock the irritation loose, the lumbering beast sauntered over to a herd of henpeckers. Part bird, part goat--the beaks on these scavengers were razor-sharp and could pick a garbage eater clean in two minutes.

Bailey scared away the henpeckers as Nick jumped onto the garbage eater's back. Rooting through the mess of tangled hair, Nick felt something lumpy. He quickly cleared away the matted growth and exposed a familiar head. The lump was his brother.

Hiding in the thick coat, Jack lay curled up into a ball, trembling. He raised his head cautiously when Nick put a hand on his shoulder.

Seeing Jack in the demented world of the game sent Nick into a kind of shock and he just stared stupidly at his older brother. The garbage eater shifted its weight and nearly clawed Jack with a clumsy but powerful arm. Nick snapped out of it, grabbed his brother and threw him off the beast.

Bailey's jaw dropped when she saw Jack. The stampede of curious creatures was almost upon them, so Nick hustled Bailey and Jack away from the garbage eater.

Nick had never seen his brother like this--cowering and afraid. His brother that had always been his hero; his brother that had once stood up to three bullies at one time; his brother that scared substitute teachers right out of the classroom.

Now, for the first time in his life, Nick actually felt sorry for Jack. That was definitely a new feeling. Seeing his hero in such a pathetic condition left him a little shaken.

Nick led them toward the next portal, unable to look at his brother. Jack walked with his head down, pulled along by Bailey. The portal appeared ahead of them, hovering above the path. Nick let Bailey go first then followed Jack through.

The fourth level shimmered darkly as they stepped off the platform. Nick knew immediately this level was nothing like the first three. No creatures were within sight, but he felt a presence so menacing it gave him chills and he instinctively took a step back. Something was there waiting for them, something that permeated the entire level and seemed to know their every move.

Jack took off running for some hills in the distance. Bailey chased after him. Nick knew there was a trap waiting for them, but followed reluctantly. The menacing presence was toying with them, controlling their direction.

As they approached the foothills, Nick felt the presence grow stronger. Just ahead of them a black spot on the ground started to pulse and grow. All the dark matter in the game seemed to converge and coagulate upon that spot, twisting and twirling like a black whirlwind. Slowly the storm took shape, rising into a form that violently absorbed all remaining dark energy. When the dust settled, there stood before them the terror of the game.

The gargoyle smiled. Then it knocked them off their feet with a slight flap of its enormous wings.

Over eight feet tall, the beast had long claws on its hands and feet, and a pair of horns twisting out of its hideous head. The monster's tail was sharp and hairy with a spike at the end. Its two bat-like wings seemed to have a life of their own. Shimmering as it moved, the beast's muscular body flowed from one dark color to another like a living suit of armor.

Jack got up and ran straight for the hills. The gargoyle swatted him like a fly and sent him sprawling. He got up and tried a different direction, but the beast knocked him to the ground again.

Jack's lost his mind, thought Nick. Being thrown into the game must have really blown his fuse. He keeps running for those hills like a mad monkey.

Nick tried to lead the gargoyle away from Jack. He ran one way and motioned for Bailey to go in the opposite direction.

The gargoyle tackled Nick first then flew lazily over to Bailey and tossed her twenty feet in the air. She landed hard and had trouble getting back on her feet.

Nick decided to change tactics and rushed the gargoyle.

He woke up in the dirt about ten feet away with little stars circling around his head. The gargoyle let out a delighted howl as Nick got up and attacked again. This time he connected, hitting the gargoyle squarely in the chest. He thought he broke his hand.

The gargoyle picked Nick up with both hands and lifted him high in the air. Nick saw Jack reach the hills, with Bailey in close pursuit. The hills floated like clouds, hovering about fifty meters in the air; beyond them was a massive thunderstorm. Nick smiled as Jack ran straight for the storm.

The gargoyle turned to see why Nick was smiling, and then let out a scream when it saw Jack running beneath the floating hills. The beast bared its fangs and threw the boy as far as he could in the opposite direction, then flew like a bullet toward Jack.

Flying past Bailey, the gargoyle gently tapped her on the back of the head, knocking her to the ground. She landed on her face. Jack was beyond the hills and almost in the heart of the storm when the beast finally reached him.

Lightning bounced all around them, electrifying the air and sending curls of smoke rising where it hit. The gargoyle seemed indestructible and moved fearlessly between the thunderous bolts of raw power. The monster knocked Jack off his feet with a powerful backhand.

As the gargoyle picked Jack up and prepared to rip him apart, Bailey surprised the creature from behind. She grabbed its tail and twisted it. The beast reached for Bailey with one hand and held Jack with the other. Suddenly, Nick came out of nowhere and wrapped himself around the gargoyle's head.

Jack wriggled free and managed to pull Bailey from the monster's grip. Nick rode the gargoyle like a wild horse, clinging tightly to its head as it thrashed blindly, trying to shake him loose. They headed deeper into the storm.

A flash of lightning split the sky and hit Jack square in the chest, knocking him off his feet. He looked down to find a bolt of lightning sitting in his lap. It was blue.

Suddenly the ground opened up and a rickety wooden outhouse rose majestically out of the dirt. Jack grabbed Bailey and threw her inside, but Nick still rode the gargoyle like a bucking bronco.

He saw what Jack had done and felt ashamed for thinking his brother was a coward. And crazy. And a mad monkey. It finally dawned on Nick that there was only one reason his older brother was here--Jack had risked his own life to enter the game and save them.

Nick timed his leap so that he landed as close to the outhouse as possible. Jack helped him to his feet and they jumped into the outhouse together.

The gargoyle clenched its fists in frustration and howled with fury.

CHAPTER FOURTEEN

Wingnut's Destiny

"It's impossible," Bunsen said.

"It's never been tried," added Beaker.

"It's hopeless," Sparks chimed in.

With a determined look on his face, Wingnut put on his goggles.

"It's my destiny!"

Penny and Marbles shared a worried look. Wingnut approached the console and began adjusting coordinates and synchronizing programs.

In the game, Jack, Nick and Bailey were all safely inside the outhouse. The gargoyle raged outside, causing minor earthquakes by pounding the ground with its fists.

Penny stood in silence, a lump growing in her throat. Although it had been her idea to enter the game and lead Nick and Bailey to safety, the mere thought terrified her. Jack went in with no hesitation. He was either the bravest person she knew or the dumbest. With Jack, it was quite possible he was both. For the first time ever, she was actually proud of him.

"They made it," Wingnut said. "Now it's up to us. No time to lose."

Sparks shook his head. "Wingnut's lost his mind."

Bunsen whispered, "He's gone loopy."

Beaker picked his nose. "He's mad with confidence."

Wingnut stopped what he was doing and stormed over to the three scientists. They scattered like frightened stinkbugs as he barked orders at them.

"Sparks, set the controls for supreme debugging."

"Yes sir," Sparks replied.

"Bunsen, clear the absorbium connector and download the makeshifter."

"Done and done," Bunsen said.

"Beaker, wipe that smile off your face and hand me the monkey wrench--we're going in."

"What smile?" Beaker asked, smiling.

The scientists dashed from one end of the lab to the other, upgrading codes, splicing circuitry and customizing programs. Wingnut went back to the main console as Penny and Marbles withdrew to a safe corner to avoid being run over.

"I've got this crazy feeling they just might pull it off," Marbles said.

Penny rolled her eyes. "If not, we're gonna have an awful lot of explaining to do."

"Sparks, reboot the security code," Wingnut commanded. "Then modify the parameters."

"You're mad!" said Sparks.

"Bunsen, activate the carbon matrix and reorder the sequence."

"Careful, Wingnut," Bunsen said. "Too much tweaking and the program will shut down."

"Don't tell me about this program, I designed this program!"

"Wasn't that right after you ate some bad shrimp?" Beaker asked.

Wingnut ignored the question.

"Beaker, on my signal, contort the vertical hold then stretch the horizontal gapping."

"I was afraid you were going to say that," Beaker replied.

"Sparks, I need those parameters modified--stat!" Wingnut shouted.

"Almost there," Sparks said, with sweat dripping from his forehead.

A thin stream of smoke leaked from the console.

"The system's building pressure." Beaker said.

"Temper those modulates!" Wingnut yelled.

"I've got a bad feeling about this," said Bunsen.

"Bunsen, lock down the power grid until I can jam the sequence."

"Lock up the what now?"

"Got it!" Sparks said.

"Now, Beaker!" Wingnut yelled.

Beaker turned a huge lever one rotation and the entire console shook so hard Penny thought it was going to explode. Thick black smoke poured from the machine as the video screen flashed and flickered.

"This thing can't take this much pressure," Bunsen warned.

"She'll pull through," said Wingnut, madly adjusting dials.

"She's gonna blow!" Beaker shouted.

"Not if I can help it," Wingnut replied.

The console bulged at the seams and shrieked in metallic pain. Then something inside the machine exploded and Wingnut slammed his fist down on the eject button. The game disc screamed across the room trailing smoke as three forms tumbled from the pulsing screen onto the floor. The trembling console sighed with relief and suddenly the room was quiet.

No one said a word as the three kids sat up and gazed around the lab in astonishment. Covered in black ooze, they coughed up little dark clouds as smoke leaked from their ears.

When Bailey saw Penny, she smiled and the room erupted with laughter.

"You did it, Wingnut," Beaker shouted. "By God, you did it."

"You crazy old buzzard!" Sparks patted Wingnut on the back.

"Congratulations," Bunsen said, shaking Wingnut's hand.

Penny hugged Bailey as Marbles put out Nick's smoldering head.

"You made it, Nick," said Marbles. "How do you feel?"

"Bonus round! Bonus round!" Nick replied happily.

"What the--"

"Bailey, talk to me," Penny demanded.

"Fifty points! Fifty points!"

Everyone stared in silence at the three smoldering kids. Bailey, Nick and Jack just stared back with wide-eyed confusion. They were out of the game, but something was wrong.

Penny put a hand on Jack. "Are you okay?"

"010110100," said Jack.

CHAPTER FIFTEEN

Programmers

"**B**onus round! Bonus round!" Nick announced with a smile.

"Professor," Marbles asked, "what's wrong with my friends?"

Wingnut took a deep breath and glanced toward the other scientists before he spoke. All three averted their eyes.

"Well," said Wingnut, "it appears that when a player gets uploaded into the game, GameMonster's operating code infiltrates their mind and reprograms the brain's natural operating system. A hostile takeover, if you will. Apparently, the GameMonster program was designed to fuse with each player and make them part of the game."

"What we're witnessing is the imprint left behind," Bunsen said. "The longer they were in the game, the stronger the imprint."

"Should wear off in a couple of days," Sparks added.

"We don't know that," Beaker said. "The damage could be irreparable."

"Horse hockey!"

"It is not!"

"The Dockendorfer Postulate clearly allows for a certain amount of recalibration without any undue consequences," Sparks said.

"But if you apply the Jenkins Principle," Beaker replied, "there's no telling what could happen."

"Ahem!" Bunsen cocked her head toward the kids, who gaped in horror at the bickering scientists.

Sparks and Beaker fell silent.

"Now, don't you worry," Wingnut said. "The regenerative powers of the human mind are staggering. Given enough time, their ripe young brains should have no problem repairing themselves."

"That's right," Bunsen said, turning to Penny and Marbles. "Your friends will be fine in a few days, but you need to get them out of here before you're discovered."

"Wingnut's right, of course," said Beaker. "Unless the code contains a built-in satellite function that allows the grafting to continue even after the player has been ejected."

Wingnut and Bunsen groaned in dismay.

"In which case, you would need to destroy the GameMonster program entirely," Sparks added.

"That's the best idea I've heard all day," said Penny.

"But that would require infiltrating the programmer's level and sabotaging the system," Bunsen said.

"It's far too dangerous," Wingnut declared.

"They'd never get past the programmers."

"Those programmers are evil."

Marbles turned to Penny. "We've got to destroy that program."

"Right. We can't allow this game to hurt anyone else," Penny said. "If I turn back and go home now, I couldn't live with myself."

"I understand," said Wingnut. "But please, be careful."

"Thanks for all your help, doc."

The professors wished the kids good luck and Sparks showed them to the stairwell that led to the programmer's level.

Rising three floors without an exit, the stairs finally emptied into a long dark corridor. At the end of the corridor, an open doorway was littered with wads of paper and plastic golf balls. Penny took a deep breath and entered the room first.

Three programmers sat at their desks within grey three-sided cubicles, punching away on computer keyboards. Their hacker nicknames were posted on the edge of each cubicle. Werm was on the left, stuffing his face with a candy bar and getting chocolate all over the keyboard. On the far right, Klik had his index finger halfway up his nose, while the programmer in the middle, Vioris, was drifting off to sleep as she typed. Penny almost laughed out loud.

"These guys don't look so tough," Marbles said, poking his head into the room.

At the sound of Marbles' voice, Vioris reflexively opened her eyes and started typing on her keyboard before she was actually awake. The other two programmers didn't even bother to look up, but continued working at their computers with bored resignation.

"Who are you and what do you want?" Werm asked.

"Maybe it's those kids the director warned us about in her latest e-memo," said Klik. He pulled his finger out of his nose and examined it closely.

"What e-memo?" Vioris asked, yawning. "I never got any e-memo."

"We need to talk to the master programmer," Penny said.

"That's me," said Werm.

"Oh, it is not," Klik said.

"Yes it is," Werm replied. "I've been the master programmer for months."

"Just because you keep saying it, doesn't make it true."

"How'd you people get in here?" Werm asked.

"Hey nerdboy," Marbles said, sounding a lot like Jack. "We'll ask the questions."

"Nerdboy? They sound like inspectors," Klik said, inching his finger back toward his nose.

"Inspectors?" Vioris asked. "Nobody told me about any inspectors."

"Uh, yeah," said Penny. "We're inspectors for the...uh, shareholders...club."

"Sounds reasonable," Vioris said.

"We've had some complaints about one of your games," Penny said.

"Impossible," said Werm.

"We understand there were some problems with the GameMonster program," Penny said.

"Oooh, that's our favorite," said Vioris.

"Pure genius." Klik's finger was now securely up his nose. "I don't mememba any pwobwems."

"Yes, well," Penny said, "it seems that every quack hacker with a Mac can break down your code, enter the system and foul up the works."

"No way. That code is a digital fortress."

"A veritable Fort Knox."

"Oh, uh...like a really sturdy fence."

Marbles tried to get a closer look and accidentally stepped on Bailey's foot.

"Fifty points! Fifty points!" Bailey cried.

"Hey, that sounds like a ditto-code imprint from the GameMonster program," said Werm.

"Bonus round! Bonus round!" Nick said.

The programmers finally looked up from their computers and realized they had not been talking to inspectors from the shareholders club.

"It's those kids the e-memo warned us about," Klik said.

"They've been in the game," Vioris squealed.

"Those e-memos are never wrong."

All at once, the three programmers scrambled out of their cubicles in a burst of panic and huddled together in a corner. They fought to hide behind each other as chairs spun and papers settled to the floor.

"I'll bet those meddling professors let them out," Werm said.

"These are the evil programmers we're supposed to watch out for?" Marbles asked.

Penny walked over to the nearest computer, but the keyboard had chocolate all over it, so she moved to the next one.

"No!" Werm said. "She mustn't be allowed on that computer."

"She could destroy everything."

"She's not a graduate of CompuTech Institute!" Vioris cried.

"Don't worry about me," Penny said, "as soon as I get rid of this nasty little program, I'll be on my way."

"Nobody's going anywhere." All heads turned at the sound of this new voice.

Evelyn Erickson strolled into the room, followed by a squadron of blank-faced technicians dressed in green. The three goofy programmers tittered nervously.

"The evil executive," said Werm.

"Ms. Chairman of the Board," said Klik.

"The cranky old fart from the fifth floor," said the other one.

Evelyn looked up at this last comment and shot the programmers a nasty look.

"Don't tell me you're afraid of a few children."

"Uh, well...no, not...yeah, we are," Werm admitted.

"I spend a fortune hiring the evilest programmers money can buy and you're worried about a few stinky kids?"

"But everyone knows that children are a nerd's worst nightmare," Werm replied.

"Hey, I am not a nerd," said Klik. "I'm a computer geek."

The corporate executive silenced the programmers with a wave of her hand then turned her attention to Penny.

"Now really, my dear," she said, approaching Penny. "What in Atari's name do you hope to accomplish on that computer?"

"I'm going to destroy this program," Penny said.

"A woman who knows her mind--impressive," Evelyn said. "But I'm afraid that's quite impossible."

"Nothing's impossible," shouted Marbles.

"Oh, how cute." Evelyn gestured toward Marbles. "Sidekick?"

"Bonus round! Bonus round!" shouted Nick.

"Ah, sounds like someone's spent time in our little game," Evelyn said, smiling. "That's music to my ears. You must be those brats that store manager warned me about."

"1001011001!" shouted Jack.

"I must say, your persistence is amazing. Now, who let you out of there, I wonder?"

"I bet it was those snooty professors in the lab," said Klik.

"Well, of course it was those snooty professors in the lab," Evelyn said, rolling her eyes. "I was being facetious...or rhetorical or something."

"That doesn't matter," Penny said. "The fact is, we're here now and we're going to do whatever it takes to destroy this program."

"Oh, you silly child," said Evelyn. "Even if you were able to get past all the programmers and technicians, you'd have no chance of destroying the program itself."

"All the programmers?" Penny laughed. "These three couldn't stop my baby sister."

"Fifty points!" agreed Bailey.

Evelyn walked over to a bank of light switches and flipped them all on.

"Not these programmers."

The lights flickered for a moment, then came on. Thousands of fluorescent lights illuminated hundreds of cubicles, bathing the entire level in an eerie flickering glare. Each cubicle held a pale programmer dressed in black, hunched over a computer keyboard, working feverishly. Reacting to the light, they shielded their eyes and bent closer to the comforting glow of the computer monitors. The programmers soon became agitated and emitted a low whining sound.

"These programmers."

Penny's mouth fell open as she peered over the cubicles, straining to see the far end of the room. Row after row of three-sided workstations filled the enormous office. Between the humming of the fluorescent lights and the whining of the programmers, the entire level vibrated with a buzzing groan. The endless honeycomb of cubicles and incessant droning gave the impression of a hive. A chill raced up her spine when the notion occurred to her. That's it. They were in some kind of crazy evil hive filled with over-achieving brainiacs working on God-knows-what.

"Unbelievable," said Marbles.

"Believe it, stinky," Evelyn said. "I've got thousands of programmers, software engineers and code-dependent eggheads working on everything from viruses to software bacteria to God-knows-what. We write enough evil code in one week to destroy all the computers in the southern hemisphere."

"Let me guess," Penny said. "You're going to unleash your unholy barrage of computer plagues on the world so that everyone will have to buy your software."

"Well, not exactly," Evelyn replied. "But that's not bad."

Evelyn snapped her fingers and the technicians descended upon the kids. It took four green men to subdue Jack.

The technicians dragged them to the center of the immense swirl of cubicles where two machines stood back to back. One was a vending machine full of chocolate and candy, the other a vintage arcade game. Gargoyles and monsters had been painted over the original artwork on the video game. GameMonster, in dripping red letters, took up one whole side.

"You seem so eager to destroy the GameMonster program, I've decided to let you give it a shot," said Evelyn. "You see, I've hidden the code for the master game program in one of the game's characters."

Marbles looked over at Vioris. "Is that possible?"

"We went through four truckloads of coffee trying to figure out how to pull that one off," she replied.

"This game is connected to the mainframe computer," Werm added. "It helps to have the actual game handy when we want to make changes to the program."

Penny stepped up to the video game. Jack struggled against the technicians.

"The only way to destroy the program is to kill the beast hiding it," Evelyn said with a smile.

"No," Marbles cried. "It's a trick."

"I have no choice," said Penny.

"That's right," Evelyn said. "You have no choice. Now, let's see how good you are at video games."

The other kids groaned in dismay as Penny put her hands on the controls and the game popped to life. A pinpoint of light grew slowly out of the center until it covered the entire screen then melted into the game logo graphics.

The game started and Penny wondered how in the world she was going to get out of this alive. A few plans formulated as the first level popped into view. She thought about knocking Evelyn to the floor, grabbing Bailey and hightailing it out of there. But there was too great a chance that someone wouldn't make it. Whatever happened, she wasn't about to leave anyone behind. She thought about offering herself in trade if Evelyn would let the others go, but there was no way to be sure the old bat would keep her word.

Soon, Penny spent less time thinking of ways to escape and more time concentrating on the game. Gradually, her surroundings faded to black, leaving only the video screen in her field of vision.

Within minutes, the game was all she cared about. Maybe she was all wrong about video games; this wasn't so bad after all. In fact, it was almost enjoyable. The game actually gave her wonderful sensations--the beauty of movement, the excitement of the chase, the giddy thrill of slaying nasty creatures.

She was being pulled in and she knew it. The first and most powerful possession was of the mind. Once the game had that, it was only a simple matter to pull in the rest of you. She could feel the game's hold on her grow stronger, but she didn't care. It made her more powerful as it took over and she had never felt power like this before.

Penny worked her way through level one, quickly mastering the controls. By the time she reached level two, she was adept at spins, kicks, flips, and corner blocks. At one point, she even pulled off a Double Rigdon when two beasts rushed at her from both sides and she managed to jump out of the way at the last minute. The two creatures disintegrated in a tangled heap.

Evelyn tried every dirty trick in the book to get Penny to make a mistake. She shouted words of discouragement at the girl. She bumped into her, accidentally on purpose. She even tried setting Penny's shirt on fire.

But Penny was oblivious to everything going on around her. She never noticed Evelyn's attempts to distract her. She didn't see the kids struggle against the strong arms of the icy technicians that held them. She couldn't feel the programmers swarming closer, nor hear their incessant droning grow louder and louder.

The only thing Penny noticed was the creature emerging from a lava tube in the game. She never took her eyes off it as it stretched its wings and roared.

CHAPTER SIXTEEN

Game Over

Goyle was about to get upset. There was a party going on and, once again, he hadn't been invited. He wanted desperately to join in the celebration, but he couldn't see over the wall of programmers.

Not too long ago, a few flaps of his wings would've sent him soaring over the crowd. But ever since they installed the candy machines, his flights have gotten shorter and shorter. Now he's lucky if his feet get off the ground at all.

He'd found the front-gate guards thrashing around in a pile like a couple of spazoids. Two maintenance guys stood around arguing about the best way to fix them. Goyle tried knocking some sense back into the guards by carefully smashing them in the head a few times, but it didn't help. He also tried propping them up on their feet, but they just toppled over again. He got tired of trying after awhile. The maintenance guys were still arguing as he headed toward the maintenance shed. They had a pretty good candy machine in there.

Unable to stand it any longer, Goyle shoved his way through the throng of programmers. The crowd parted with no resistance whatsoever.

"Oh boy, a party," said Goyle, as he reached the center of the circle.

Marbles' mouth fell open when he saw the gargoyle step out of the crowd. Jack, Bailey and Nick all recoiled in terror, assuming he was the same monster they had eluded in the game.

Goyle turned to the programmer next to him. "Where's the cake?"

"Oh great, look who's here," said the programmer.

"It's the company mascot."

"The concrete icon."

"The great brain."

The crowd of programmers erupted in laughter. Unaware that they were laughing at him, Goyle soon joined in with great whoops and howls. Stamping his feet with delight sent massive shock waves rumbling across the floor.

When he calmed down, Goyle looked around the room and saw the kids for the first time.

The crowd fell silent as Goyle approached Evelyn cautiously.

"Hey boss," Goyle said. "Whatcha doin' there, boss?"

Evelyn was too busy harassing Penny to hear him.

"Hey boss, I think I found them kids you was looking for."

Goyle was just about to tap Evelyn on the shoulder when Marbles finally spoke.

"Excuse me...sir?"

Goyle turned his head slightly.

"Yuh?"

"Aren't you the guy on those TV commercials?"

Goyle looked Marbles up and down before answering.

"Yeah."

"Are you really a gargoyle?"

Goyle's face darkened and his eyes got all squinty.

"Yeh."

Marbles hesitated a moment as he put on a thoughtful expression, then suddenly broke into his trademark smile.

"Man, I love those commercials! I think you're awesome!"

Goyle's eyes lit up and his face brightened into a smile. It wasn't everyday that someone complimented him on his acting. He whirled around to meet his new friend and his tail smacked Evelyn in the back of the head.

As Goyle shook Marbles' hand, Evelyn fell forward but managed to stay on her feet by grabbing onto the video game. Regaining her balance, Evelyn straightened up to see a new character appear onscreen. She stared in confusion at the monitor then lowered her gaze to find her right hand wrapped firmly around the second-player joystick.

The beast in the game howled.

Evelyn barely had time to look surprised before she disintegrated into the screen. A muted gasp seemed to hang in the air along with millions of her colorful molecules. Then, in a flash of leopard skin, she was gone.

And so was Penny.

As Evelyn's essence fell into the game, Penny hesitated for a split second. But that was all the gargoyle needed to pull her into its violent world.

Programmers stared dumbfounded as Goyle turned around cautiously to see what he'd done. The technicians relaxed their grip on the kids, who took the opportunity to squirm free.

Penny was disoriented, but knew immediately where she was. She also knew that this was her last chance. The beast would come for her now, stronger than ever. Her only hope was to catch it off guard, and that was almost impossible. She would never be able to surprise it; the creature was always two steps ahead and twice as fast. Eventually, the gargoyle would catch up to her and destroy her.

Just as she was about to give up, the answer came to her. Like a flash of lightning in her cloudy head. She knew what to do.

Run.

So she ran. She ran leaving Evelyn confused and staggering in her dust. She ran with the gargoyle just behind her and gaining every minute. She ran like Bailey from a soccer-game rumble.

Penny ran until she saw the portal to the next level hovering a few feet off the ground. Without missing a beat, she dove onto the portal and the next level materialized instantly.

Unfortunately, the gargoyle materialized right along with it.

The beast stood there waiting for her to jump off the platform. It waited with a deadly grin, saliva dripping from its fangs. Huge muscles tensed and twitched as it anticipated her leap from the platform.

But Penny didn't move. The gargoyle looked confused and feigned a grab for her. She flinched but held her ground.

The monster twitched and jerked with bloodlust, unsure of what to do next. Waiting was not its strong suit and thinking was practically out of the question. It was the beast of the game, the destroyer. It destroyed things. It was time to destroy this one.

The gargoyle spread its wings wide and lunged with lightning speed. At that exact moment, Penny stepped off and the gargoyle landed with a thud on the empty platform, its claws cutting deep gashes into the surface. Time ran out as the beast tensed for another leap and the platform exploded.

The game flickered on and off and the entire console shook violently. Suddenly, the screen went black.

Goyle heard a terrible howling sound fill the room. It took a minute before he realized he was the one howling.

After a moment of frozen shock, the crowd scattered. Programmers scrambled over each other in a mad dash to get back to the safety of their cubicles. The mysterious technicians disappeared silently into the chaos.

Marbles and Jack started toward the game but Goyle grabbed them and gently held them back. Staying with the kids, the three goofy programmers tittered and frittered worriedly. No one took their eyes off the game machine shaking quietly in the center of the room, and no one approached it. Even the candy machine seemed to move away.

As the seconds ticked by, the air hung heavy with a sinking feeling that it was finished. The game was over and nobody could do anything about it.

Marbles thought about all the times Penny stood up for him. Jack remembered being jealous of Penny because she could run faster than he could; it didn't seem to bother him so much now. Bailey pictured life without her older sister, and started to cry. Nick thought back to all the times Penny lifted his spirits after Jack had humiliated him in public. Goyle thought about all that candy in that machine over there.

But then the game console burped softly and brought everyone's attention back to it. Silently, as if breathing, the machine pulsed in and out of focus. The game hiccuped rapidly and then exploded with hurricane force into a million pieces. The three programmers were knocked off their feet, but Goyle spread his wings wide protecting the kids from the debris.

In a cloud of dust, two shaking black forms rose where the machine had been. Covered in soot, with smoke curling off her head, Penny held Evelyn in her arms.

The kids swarmed around Penny, knocking Evelyn to the floor. The dazed executive landed hard on her butt.

"Penny," Marbles said, cleaning the soot off her face. "Speak to me."

They leaned in close waiting for her reply. Penny blinked a few times then took a deep breath.

"I hate video games."

They all laughed and hustled toward the exit. Penny took one last look over her shoulder.

Goyle stuffed a candy bar in his mouth and waved goodbye. Evelyn sat on the floor in a heap as the three programmers tried to put out her smoldering head. When she saw Penny's glance, she raised her arm defiantly.

"□□□□□□□□□□," shouted Evelyn.

CHAPTER SEVENTEEN

The Road Home

Penny led the group down from the programmer's level and out of the building. They made their way through the ruined gate, up the valley and onto the highway that led back to town.

The sun was getting low in the sky and painted the evening pink and orange.

They were tired and dirty. No one spoke as they trudged down the highway, keeping an eye out for familiar landmarks. Bailey held Penny's hand as they walked. Jack and Nick marched in unison, affectionately punching each other. Marbles brought up the rear.

Penny smiled to herself. She was overcome with a strange new sensation; it may have been pride, she wasn't quite sure. They did it. They worked together as a team and they won--first time ever.

"Bleep."

A shiver ran up Penny's spine. She thought she heard a video game. But that's crazy. The game was destroyed. Must be her nerves playing tricks on her.

"Blip."

Impossible. Not after all they'd been through. Maybe it was an aftershock from all the stress.

"Bloop."

Penny stopped and turned slowly around.

The gang was ragged and tired, dragging themselves along the road behind her. They turned to see what she was staring at.

Shuffling toward them with his head lowered, Marbles held something in front of his face. Every so often, the thing in his hands let out an electronic giggle.

Marbles didn't notice his friends staring at him in wide-eyed horror. He was too busy lunging and dodging and leaping for his life, battling game-monsters on a portable Pocket Player.

Blip. Bloop. Bleep.

The End

ABOUT THE AUTHOR

David Marti spent some time trapped inside a video game, but never made it past level one. A reclusive curmudgeon given to spontaneous fits of absurdity, he lives on an island and raises jellyfish in his bathtub.